POISON AND WINE

Poison and Wine
Dust to Dust

POISON AND WINE
(Book One of the Poison and Wine series)
C.H. Valentino and Eldon Hughes

Visit: www.chvalentino.com and www.ifoundaknife.com

Published by Valentino Books Inc.
Cover art by Stephanie Thompson

To Deb and Cole,
who make our worlds complete.

Authors' Notes

by C.H. Valentino

First, thank you. If you're stopping to read these few paragraphs, you're helping to fulfill a lifelong dream, and that makes this a very intimate moment for you and me. And since we're good friends now, and I should tell you a secret:

I am in love with this book.

Dante Alighieri once wrote: "A mighty flame follows a tiny spark." That is exactly how this began. It was a writing exercise. No more than a breath blown over the embers of a creative imagination. Next thing I knew, we were fifty pages in and looking at a world we were both decidedly too in love with to simply walk away.

Now, it's not often that I am allowed to get smooshy, but we should all be so lucky to have friendships in our lives born out of shared interest. In Eldon, I have found a confidant most profound, often infuriating, but generally only when he is demanding my best. I never get to tell him how much *fun* I had writing this book. I certainly don't get to extol his virtues as my friend, nor do I get to tell him how grounding it is to know another writer who can reach into my mind and pluck out the exact words I was thinking. You made me so mad. It was magic. It still is.

That said, the road to self-publishing wasn't magic. It was hard as hell and I would have never gotten through it without tutorial gurus Gwen Hernandez, Garrett Robinson and Ed Ditto. All three of them are pretty damn fine authors in their own right, so I would be remiss in not recommending them to you now. A special nod to Garrett, who has unknowingly been my crutch for many months now. Staples, man. Staples. Also, incredible thanks to Christy Brock and Paige Crutcher, who were the only two people who made it through very early, very rough drafts of this thing. Your notes were priceless.

Finally, in pursuit of this book, our spouses indulged us by giving up many hours of our company. They listened as we argued and laughed about things that I'm certain made no sense at the time. They delivered us cups of tea and plates of cookies, kissed us, and left us to our madness. And when this book was over, they let us do it again. You could not ask for two more selfless people than Deb and Cole, and I cannot express the depth of my thanks to either of them. Deb, you are, without a doubt, a true friend. Thank you for lending me your husband. Spoon, I love you.

By Eldon Hughes

What she said.

Prologue

Sister Martine had always liked this part of the evening best.

Sun went down, streets cooled off. The air lost its diesel edge and grew rich with the smell of slow-smoked meat. Time was, children played in the streets of the Ninth Ward any time of day. But not lately. It seemed she had lost their days to video games and their nights to gangs. Now, all she had of them was the blue-gray gap in between.

She swung a pair of jump ropes for a double-dutch crew. They cut wide, whooping slices through the air. The younger children rushed through the center, catching their foot on the back end of the rope before stumbling out. One by one, sometimes two at a time, Sister Martine's happy laughter chased them across the asphalt and back to the end of the line.

The girl on the other end dropped the rope. She turned and started off down the road.

Confused, Sister Martine called after her.

"Chartrese, where you going?"

Chartrese didn't answer, and wherever she was going,

all of the other children went with her. They marched off in a loose herd, away from the game and deeper into the dusky twilight.

"Chartrese! Deshaune!" Sister Martine called again. "Where are you going?"

"Can't you hear the music, Sister?" they asked.

She couldn't, which made her walk that much faster.

The last bit of light slipped from the sky. In no time at all she was chasing shadows in the dark, flashes of faces moving around one corner and the next. The faster they walked, the faster she followed. By the time she reached the dead-end of the street, they had all vanished.

Sister Martine stopped, listened, and looked back. The street was just wide enough for one car and the tenement houses leaning over it. Hurricane Katrina had taken out the street lamps, but at what point the buzz of crickets had stopped, she couldn't say. The silence made the street feel gravely empty.

She started forward again when she caught a glimpse of Chartrese between the alley. The pavement turned to gravel and then grass as Sister Martine hurried forward through a vacant lot. Evening dew soaked her habit and the soft soles of her shoes. She slid to a stop on the edge of the yard.

The children had gathered against a battered wooden fence that separated the adjoining alley from the street. The only way back would be the way she came. She didn't know why, but the thought stole her breath and she reached to the rosary on her hip.

The children began to sing.

"Talkin' bout hey now. Hey now! Iko Iko an deye."

It was a simple song. She'd taught it to most of them herself. But there was no joy in their faces as they sang out each refrain.

A tall shadow slipped over her. Startled, she turned to find an equally tall man in the mouth of the alley. His face stayed in the darkness, but his voice crept out across her skin.

"Jockamo fe nah ah nay."

Light flashed against the face of a heavy, gold coin as he rolled it across the back of his knuckles. She glanced back at the children. Their song was getting louder.

"Iko, Iko an deye! Jockamo fe nah ah na nay! Jockamo fe nah ah nay!" they sang.

"What are you doing to them?" she demanded.

"Just treating them to a little show," the man said.

"A show?"

Suddenly, Sister Martine realized he was no longer looking at her, but past her. She smelled mud again, wet and heady, but also blood.

The man tossed the coin high into the air. A second shadow descended over the grass, this time between her and the children. It snuffed out the remaining light, and then their voices one by one.

Sister Martine wrenched her hand around her rosary.

"Lord, save us all."

One

Danni propped a slender arm behind her head while the other sat loosely against her stomach. Her tongue was thick with the cloying taste of champagne. The empty bottle lay against the deck, rocking idly against the wood. She'd only planned to have one glass, but one had turned to two, then three, and finally the might-as-well chug that left her feeling boneless and warm.

The steamboat lurched into deeper waters. Paddles struck the dark Mississippi with a hard, percussive slap, almost enough to cover the mechanized whine of the diesel engine that drove them. Nothing was truly steam-driven anymore, and certainly not the *Maribelle*, which was lucky to run even one of her three boasted BEST NIGHTLY TOURS IN NEW ORLEANS.

The ballroom doors swung open, wafting out a fresh blast of conditioned air and the boxy squeal of a trumpet before falling shut again. Two college students positioned themselves against the skyline and snapped a quick picture with a cellphone before darting back inside.

Others trickled in and out. Newlyweds. Not-so-newlyweds. A group of sailors in their pressed whites. They paused to mock the staged rigging on the lifeboats, tossing a few loose glances in Danni's direction until eventually all but one of them returned to the bar.

His uniform was pristine white and finished with a matching Dixie hat. He kept his eyes on her but stayed at the starboard rail. Danni stood and walked the length of the deck, letting him keep pace until she set her chin against her shoulder and called to him.

"Where y'at, sailor?"

It was all the invitation he needed. He crossed to meet her with a glint of mischief in his blue eyes, pulling the hat from his head and running a hand through a damp shag of blond hair.

"Ma'am." He gripped the rail beside her. "Lovely night."

"Is it?" She settled her fingers into the crease of his elbow. "I hadn't noticed."

His pulse thrummed against her palm, bringing hundreds of loose details as his life unwound quickly across her mind. A whisper of conversation, followed by heated words and harder smacks.

"Dean Carlton. Nineteen with an ID that says you're twenty-two," she said, "but no head for whiskey. A few broken hearts, more broken noses."

His astonishment quickly melted to suspicion, and his hand clamped down around her wrist.

"My buddies tell you that?" he snarled.

They hadn't needed to. Danni could feel the anger in his soul.

Danni rocked herself forward and laid her lips against his. Though chaste, the kiss stilled the air between them, blocking out the hum of the engine and the ripple of water.

Her free hand moved into the slim pocket of her sundress and twitched around the handle of a blade.

Raw magic called to the anger in his touch. Dean's eyes widened. Goosebumps stippled his flesh, sinew flexing against the pressure of his soul as it was pulled across her skin, out of him and into her.

The tense, angry lines of Dean's forehead released to form softer plains. As the last of his soul seeped away, his grip relaxed and his hand fell against his hip. The mischief had left his eyes permanently. With a vacant stare, he staggered away from Danni and back toward the bar.

She pulled herself straight and tried to shake off the dull throb of the champagne before flipping the blade over in her fist.

"Holy crap, it's hot."

The sudden voice startled her. The knife thudded against the deck. She spun to face a man who looked just as startled as she felt. His eyes darted back and forth between her and the blade wedged between the slats.

"You dropped your knife."

He bent to retrieve it before turning it over in his fist a few times.

"Interesting carving on the handle," he said. "Can't really make out the shapes." He held it up to the light. "Some kind of writing. What does it say?"

Danni wet her lips and shrugged.

The moonlight bent off the knife and across his eyes. It ignited the flecks of silver and gold near the center of his iris. There was something strangely attractive about his face. Not the hopeful glimmer of a sailor or the doe-eyed fascination of a tourist, but the subtle discipline of a man who either didn't care or had bigger problems than a stranger with a knife.

"Champagne?" he offered.

The bottle he produced was the brand from the bar, the same she'd already had, which meant he'd noticed her long before this "chance" encounter. How long had he been waiting, working up the courage to approach her? He used the knife to wedge the cork out of the bottle.

"Ladies first."

She watched the condensation roll down the cool, green glass. Wordlessly, she raised the bottle to her lips and took a long swallow. As she lowered it, his eyes darted out to the water and waited for hers to follow. When she looked back, the knife was gone.

She stepped into him but kept the bottle between them. She pressed it against his belly and waited for him to take it. When he did, her fingers slid up his chest and stopped against his heart.

The first wave of heat pulsated into her hand, down her arm, and into her lungs. The sensation flooded her senses with a blinding, frantic whiteness, like a blizzard in the center of a warm spring. She took a short breath then a deeper one. She searched the chaos but couldn't find a single image in the maelstrom, not a sound or a word. Not even his name.

The deck shifted as the *Maribelle* caught the wake of a passing barge. Danni staggered back and the man caught the rail. They both struggled for air. She knew his gasps: fear. Hers felt more like hunger.

Who the hell was he? And the more relevant question: if she couldn't steal his soul, how was she going to get her knife back?

He lifted the bottle again and spread his arms wide.

"To the nightmares that keep us awake." He brought the bottle to his lips, swallowed deeply, and smiled. "And the monsters we no longer wish to be."

He offered her the bottle again. She had no toasts to make, certainly nothing as ominous as his. The bubbles buzzed inside her mouth as she swallowed once, twice, and a third time until she could hold her breath no longer. She braced her elbows on the rail's edge and swung the bottle over the Mississippi.

"They say there are fish the size of sedans this far down stream," she said. "Swallow a man whole, if they could. Only real monsters left in New Orleans, I think."

"Would that it were true," he said. "I'd spend my days fishing the rivers instead of the shore."

He took the bottle from her again, put a thumb over top, and shook it up and down.

"Neat thing about bubbly. It does just what we call it. *Bubbles*." He moved his thumb, and a stream of champagne shot out across the water. "Right about now you're feeling it bubbling inside you. Let it come. Wait. Don't try to run. You'll hurt yourself falling."

Danni felt his eyes on her as she slid down the railing. Her head sank toward the deck as numbness crept over her face, spilling down her arms with tingling warmth as her mind unwound around the last few minutes.

Silver light split across her narrowing vision. The knife flashed forward in his fist. *Her* knife. Her arm came up to stop him but didn't make the reach and instead, she caught the loose crotch of his painter's pants.

He caught her hand easily. "Careful now."

The blade caught the moonlight for just a moment before disappearing over the rail.

Danni struggled for each breath, dimly aware that whatever he'd given her might not leave her enough strength to breathe.

Gently, he slid his arms beneath her knees and cradled a hand behind her head. The ship's horn sounded. A gentle thud made the deck shudder beneath his feet.

A voice cried over the loudspeakers. "All ashore!"

He carried her to the gangway. The tour guide at the top asked after her. Danni fought to open her eyes. Whoever this was, whatever had happened, she was far from okay.

"Girlfriend's had a bit much, is all," the man holding her said. "G'night."

His footfalls were heavy. The shifting motion of the dock faded as he transitioned from wood to solid ground. Danni's thoughts submerged deeper until she lost the stiff brush of his shirt against her face and the sway of his steps. And then there was nothing at all.

Two

Most people found themselves in *Chautain Rue* by taking a couple of wrong turns off Bourbon Street, which made sense. There were as many wrong turns as right ones in the French Quarter.

Those who made their way inside found exactly what they expected to: a small room that wasn't too bright or too clean filled with overpriced Mardi-Gras commemoratives. Gaudy plastic beads, tiny plastic voodoo statues, and cheap t-shirts from last year's parades, all screaming "Where y'at!" and "Show us your TITS!"

The dreadlocked kid behind the counter barely looked up from his graphic novel as Michael pushed a row of t-shirts aside and moved through the doorway behind them.

The transition from kitchen to craft was immediate. Broken down to its raw components, the makings of magic looked a lot like a collection from a farmer's market. Bundled herbs, straw, and chickens' feet hung from the low rafters. Michael lifted a pale green glass jar from the table. Whatever the hairy thing inside was, it had been dead a long time.

"Hey, St. Mikey! What's shaking?"

The voice was more suggestion than sound, a deep, ominous bass, floating up from somewhere below and behind him.

Startled, Michael turned a few quick circles in search of him. "Dammit, Joto! Where are you?"

"I'm in the back. Chill. I'll be out in a minute."

A door closed somewhere down the hall. Michael heard the sound of rubber wheels on warped wood before Joto rolled into view.

John Todd Margolin went to Desert Storm a six-foot college football hero and came home a four-foot paraplegic. But the t-shirt stretched across his massive chest and powerhouse arms read 'I don't need feet to kick your ass.'

And that about summed it up.

"See you got some new shirts," Michael said.

Joto frowned. "Fuck you. Tacky shit pays the power bills."

"You got my stuff?"

"Brown sack on the counter over there."

Michael tentatively opened the bag and pushed the contents around for a better look.

"Hey, you wanna grope it, you gotta buy it first."

"Sure thing. A hundred, right?" Michael asked.

"It was one-fifty this morning."

Michael unfolded a few bills from his jeans and tossed them over the table. "Thanks for hooking me up."

"Happy to help a brother in arms. Is this for her?"

Michael nodded and scrubbed a hand across his jaw. "She had a weird reaction to the sedative last night."

"You *doped* her?" Joto's eyebrows crowded down around the bridge of his nose. "Wait a minute, you didn't use that *dòmi poud* I gave you, did ya?"

11

Michael winced. "One, you said sleeping powder. Two, she had a knife."

"Still, not the best way to recruit help."

Joto jerked the paper bag out of his hands and pointed him toward a row of bottles on the opposite wall.

"Hand me the green one on the end."

Michael hustled to retrieve it. Joto ticked out a few shakes of white powder into the bottom of the sack, refolded the top of the bag, and slid it back to Michael.

"Pop it in some juice before you give it to her. Now, *spill.*"

Michael footed the stool from the end of the table and sat. He folded his hands together and pressed them to his lips.

"She's… fierce. Powerful. You can sense there's something exciting about her."

"Exciting, the man says." Joto flattened his hands on the table. Spread out, they looked like tree roots, gnarled and ashen in the creases of his knuckles. "Is she hot?"

Michael eyes snapped up. "Excuse me?"

"Is she hot?" he pressed. "Don't tell me those nuns were right, and you finally went blind."

Michael blew a long breath out through his nose. She was more than hot. After a week of watching her from a distance, when he'd finally seen her up close, it had taken a great deal of effort not to mention exactly how much she reminded him of the sculpted angels in Metairie Cemetery. White skin stretched over delicate bone, offset by thick, dark hair he could still smell on his shirt.

Michael shook the thought from his head.

"Blind wouldn't have made a difference. When she touched me it was like some kind of liquid fire poured into my chest."

Joto's grin was gone. "Are you okay?"

Michael shook off his concern. "She was just trying to distract me to get her knife back."

"*Back?*"

"Yeah." He dumped the blade on the table between them. "It's kind of cool. Check out the crazy markings on the handle."

The carvings were clearer in the light but not any easier to decipher. They ran down both sides of the bone handle: a twisted arrow at the bladed end and a pair of interlocking V shapes near the bottom of the hilt. In between, a crude skull and a slanted S.

"Can you make anything of that?" Michael asked.

"Not me, brother. Not my knife."

Joto held up his hands, but Michael wasn't sure who he was trying to convince.

Joto continued. "That's a voodoo blade, man. That is, it was made for a purpose, and if you ain't that purpose, you don't want to be holdin' it."

Michael shrugged and slid it back into his pocket. "Well, so far all I've seen it do is open a bottle."

Joto stared at him, wide-eyed, and then chuckled. "Michael, you know how they say God watches out for children and fools?"

Michael nodded.

"Well, he must have assigned a whole battalion of angels to cover your ass."

"I hope so. Way things look in the Ninth, I'm gonna need 'em."

"Speakin' of, you check in at home this morning?" Joto asked.

Michael hadn't. He'd been too busy. But something in Joto's tone, the way he'd asked, told Michael he should

13

have at least called.

"Sister Martine," Joto said. "Couple a folks say she was playing jump rope with the kids last night. Ain't no one seen her since."

Fresh dread filled Michael's gut.

Sister Martine made number five. Five Sisters of Mt. Carmel gone as if they'd simply evaporated off the streets. He was well past believing their disappearances were coincidence but not beyond hope that they were still alive, which is why he'd turned to Joto in the first place.

Michael pushed himself away from the table and pocketed the bag.

"I'd better get back," he said.

"Yeah, well, if there's anything else I can do for you, you know it's yours. Hey, how 'bout a *jou-jou*? On the house. I found this houngan over in a swamp near Blanche Bay, who –"

Michael waved him off. "Not this time, man. Not yet, anyway. But if things don't work out I might just…"

"Look, if you can recruit this girl, you keep her close, all right? And if you need me, you know where to find me."

"I'll see ya'."

Joto's voice caught him at the door. "If you don't, I'll come looking."

Michael believed him.

"Thanks."

Three

Sleep wasn't sleep when it was *sleeping off*. A barge horn blasted from somewhere in the near distance and shook Danni to full awareness.

The cement beneath her was warm and dry, but her body begged for something softer. She lifted a shaky hand to rub her eyes and then drew up her knees up to her chest.

Wherever she was, the windows had been blackened. The only light fell from a single, fluorescent bulb overhead. She could smell the swamp, a damp, mossy pulse of rotten vegetation. At least she was still close to the river.

A voice crept out of the darkest edge of the room. "Hungry?"

The thought of food, the smell of it, sent her stomach through the floor and back again, erupting in a long, vile gag that smelled vaguely like alcohol. She coughed and sputtered.

That voice. Why did she know that voice? Her mind searched frantically for an answer.

"Okay, no food." He stepped from the darkness to the light and extended a tall glass full of dark sludge. "Hair of the dog? I promise you'll feel better."

Whether it was the booze, the drugs, or the combination of the two, she didn't remember him being quite so tall, or tan. Exhaustion pulled the lines in his face taut and thinned his green eyes to slits. As her memory began to surface through the gossamer haze, she knew he'd been wearing the same outfit the last time she'd seen him: a black A-line shirt tucked into loose painter's pants topped with an open linen shirt.

He knelt beside her and offered the glass again. "Come on. It's not like you could feel worse, right?"

She lifted it to her mouth, but stopped.

"Why?"

He nodded once at the glass. "Drink it, then we can talk."

She did, slow at first and then almost too quickly. It was some blended cocktail of fruit she couldn't immediately identify but was suddenly too thirsty to care. The thickness of it hit her stomach hard. When she finished, he withdrew the glass from her hands and set it on the floor beside them.

She tried to will the blood to move into her limbs but felt like anything resembling dexterity had been replaced with mud. She sat up and stretched her shoulders, moving around for the first time in…

"How long?" she asked.

"Working on twenty hours now. Not as long as it probably feels to you, but then again, that stuff is different for some people."

Twenty hours. Not long enough to be missed, but just long enough to feel the first twinge of real panic. Twenty hours washed out by a stranger who, despite his cautious distance, had done a damn fine job of completely robbing her of all control and filling that space with fear.

She stared at the exposed beams overhead. Old iron water and steam pipes wove between the joists. There was at least one floor above them. As for the door… the single overhead light didn't reach the outlying walls, and she couldn't see it.

"Where are we?" she asked.

"Space I borrowed for a couple days. I wanted somewhere private we could talk after you slept off that *dòmi poud*."

His Creole needed work, which meant the street-corner houngan who gave him a sleeping curse, hadn't explained how to pronounce it, much less how it worked.

He tossed his chin toward a sun-bleached card table against the far wall, dismally small inside a room so big. A white paper bag and two Styrofoam cups sat in the middle.

"You sure you're not hungry?"

When she didn't answer, he moved to retrieve them anyway. She patted the inside pocket of her dress. Empty. The knife was gone. She tried to push back the horror of that knowledge but kept envisioning it in the mud of the Mississippi, irretrievable.

He tugged the edge of his pant leg before squatting down beside her again. His expression was soft and somewhat apologetic as he held out another cup.

"Coffee?"

He waited for her to take the first sip from the cup and then dropped the paper bag on the floor in front of her.

"And beignets," he said. "You got a name?"

"You don't know?"

He tipped his head, and the light turned the gray-green of his eyes almost silver. "Of all the things I've learned about you over the past week, no. No one seems to know your name."

Because no one needed to. Still…

"You've been watching me."

"Best as I could. You're pretty quick." He pressed a hand to his chest. "Michael."

Her stomach pulled her attention to the food beside her. She stared at the grease bleeding through the bag, watching it grow and spread for a few silent moments.

Michael nudged it forward a few inches. "Go on."

Danni fished out a beignet but kept her eyes on him. It disappeared in two bites, washed back with the last of the coffee.

Michael stared at her with a look of open curiosity. "Did you even enjoy that?"

"Hard to enjoy anything when you feel like your head's full of marbles."

She tried to stand, but the pain tossed her back onto her butt against the floor. She rubbed a hand against the back of her skull.

"Unexpected side effect. Sorry." Michael braced one foot against the floor, outstretched the other, and leaned back on his palms. "Can I know your name now?"

"Danni."

"That your real name?"

She shrugged. "Danielle."

He smiled. "Means *God is my judge*. In Hebrew, anyway."

"Danni's fine."

They stared at each other for a long minute.

"On the boat, before I walked up," he began softly, "What did you do to that sailor?"

"Not your business."

Danni pulled in a deep breath. The brief taste of Michael's soul was still under her skin, echoing back in soft, white waves. Who was he?

"Why?" she asked again.

He ran a quick hand through his red hair. "I know some people who need your help."

She blew out an exasperated breath. "How did you find me?"

"A friend named Joto."

She searched her memory for the name, but came back empty. "Don't know him."

"Didn't suspect you would. He, like a lot of people 'round here, thinks you're a ghost." He shrugged. "Either way, it's not him who needs your help. It's the sisters."

"Sisters?"

"Of Mt. Carmel."

"Nuns." Danni shook her head and scrubbed a hard hand against her eyes. "I especially don't work for nuns. Nothing personal, just that vow of poverty thing."

Michael reached around into his pocket and tossed out a stack of cash. It landed loosely between them and, from what she could tell, was mostly crisp hundreds.

"That what you're looking for? Money's not hard."

His smile faded as he stared at his empty hands. "Couple weeks ago, a few of them disappeared. Just... gone off the street."

"Don't you folks usually call the police for this stuff?"

"We did, but all the local cops can do is help look. And quietly, because it hasn't really hit the Quarter yet. Probably won't be allowed to, either. Spooks the tourists."

"And you think they need me because…"

"Can't say I know exactly *what* you are, but I know a predator when I see one. Just like I know you've been looking at that wall, trying to decide if it's the door and if you're going to have to bash my head in to get to it."

He tossed a thumb at the darkness over his shoulder. "It is and you don't."

"You'll let me go? Just like that?" she asked.

He nodded once.

"Why go to all this trouble? Why knock me out, carry me all this way?"

Michael held up a single finger. "In my defense, I thought it would just make you sleepy. You know, maybe enough not to stab me outright."

"Speaking of which, I'll need my knife back."

His face stayed unreadable, which confirmed *exactly* where her knife was.

Angry, Danni pushed herself upright and shook off the stiffness in her shoulders before stooping back down to snatch the money.

She looked him up and down a final time.

"Michael, is it? You just bought yourself a free pass. Stay away from me, or you'll find out exactly what I did to that sailor."

Halfway across the room, a bolt of pain hit her. It stabbed through her inner thigh and wound its way up to her hip. She tried to push through it, keep focus on the door. Another lance of pain split her vision, filling the center of it with a blinding white as the edges swam with darkness.

She heard her name over the steady whirl of blood in her ears. But it wasn't Michael. It was a voice edged with fury, piped up from deeper places than the concrete beneath her feet. A third bolt of pain hit her, followed by another, and with no time to brace for the next, she collapsed to the floor.

White-hot fire roared against her skin. She might have screamed, but it was lost under the deafening roar of her pulse as it slammed out a fatally slow rhythm.

Too much. It was too much! She heard her name again. The sound and the pain met in the center of her chest. Her breath left her lungs.

Her senses reeled back across the cool cement. With nothing to hold on to, no way to stop it, Danni begged for darkness to take her.

Four

Firelight lit the Spanish moss hanging from the low cypress branches. The fire flared, bringing with it the hiss and pop of leaves as they fell into the open flames. Danni stared out over the open swamp waters into New Orleans on a blue-black night, moonless but pale.

When she stepped forward, her heels sank into the mud. She hooked her ankle back and glared at the soiled soles. Purple rhinestones twinkled across the bridge of her foot and spanned the length of the heels. Pretty, if horribly impractical.

Her dress was made of layers of black silk. But the longer she stood, the more she could feel it shifting around her. She tried to rake it from her skin, but each time she seemed to find purchase on one fold the rest would slither from her grasp. A black snake lifted its head from its free roam around her waist, eyeing her with a sliver of yellow curiosity.

Snakes. It always had to be snakes.

Now that she knew she was dreaming, willing her mind to wake shouldn't be too hard. She tried to draw back the scents and sights of the warehouse, the dusky room and all its thrift-shop components. Her eyes pinched out the light as she pleaded with herself to just *wake up*.

"Oh, it's a little more than a dream, *cher*."

The scent of burning cloves stung her nose while the spell of his voice rolled her eyes back in her head. Heavy fingers danced around her waist in ten-key time, leaving trails of ash where they touched. Beneath his brocade jacket she felt the body that was neither real nor hallucination moving independent of its joints.

Fable suggested he fashioned himself from the souls of the dead, borrowing their skeletons to knit himself together. He twisted her to face him. Smoke roiled from between his teeth, an open-mouthed smile spread across his lips.

"*Akeyi yo*, Baron Samedi," she said.

Whether it was his name on her lips or the language most ancient to him, the perfume of his power increased. He lifted and twirled them across the grass while his mouth strayed to the hollow of her throat. She could feel his voice in her bones.

"I've been looking for you all day. *Where have you been?*"

There was venom in his last question, a heated threat beneath the words. She wasn't allowed to hide from him. It was part of their deal.

Her breath shuddered as the Baron's hands made a slow journey down the length of her dress. Under his touch, the snake skin turned to silk. He palmed her rib cage, fingers settling below her breast, less of a caress and more of a reminder of just how much he controlled her. A single, pointed fingernail came to rest just above the center of her chest.

"*Danielle*." The Baron spun a lazy circle against her

skin. "I will not ask you again."

The pain was dull at first, like a bruise blossoming in the space below her throat. It intensified as he wound the circle tighter.

Where should she begin? The boat? The warehouse? *Michael.*

The lingering sweetness of his soul was still on the edge of her memory, full and soft, like something she could wrap herself in.

The Baron tensed. He snapped and it sounded like bone breaking on gravel. Danni flinched. A green flash formed a vaporous cloud that slowly coalesced into Michael's face. The Baron's cool fingers slid up to her neck and seized the soft points of her throat. His voice rumbled in her ear.

"And *who* is this?"

"I - I'm not sure. He said something about a job. Some nuns who need help—"

Her words clamped off as the Baron drove his fingers into the spaces between her ribs. It was a pain she was certain would have rendered her unconscious. But here, in the part of her mind he controlled, she only suffered.

"He's been following me! I don't know why! He said someone named Joto sent him," she begged. "Please, Baron!"

All at once, he withdrew. The pain vanished and she sank forward onto her knees, gasping for a clean breath.

"Well, well. I suppose this changes everything,"

The Baron cocked one patent-leather shoe against a mossy boulder and slung the rest of his body forward over his knee. A rat snake the length and width of a shoe-string wove its way around his fingers.

What had changed, she didn't know, but his anger had turned into a vulpine grin. His gaze centered on the misty image of Michael's face.

She glanced at it, then back at the Baron.

"I - I'm not sure I understand," Danni said slowly.

"Oh, *cher*, but you do. You tasted his soul, *non?*"

He watched her face for recognition but she had none to give. He flicked the rat snake from his hand.

"You seem to have found a man of pure heart. A rarity in this city, I assure you."

He edged closer to Michael's image. "A very good choice."

"Choice for *what?*"

A finger caught the bottom of her chin, lifting it to expose the line of her throat as his breath rolled over her cheeks.

"I have a new task for you, *cher*."

The patch of earth beneath her began to undulate. The dew-soaked grass became a tangled length of eyes and scales moving smoothly around her ankles. The snakes climbed over the backs of her knees, above and below the hem of the dress. Danni swallowed hard.

The Baron set a thoughtful finger against his mouth and thumbed the half-spent rum runner in the corner of his lip.

"Join this knight's quest to protect the poor, unfortunate sisters of New Orleans. In fact, I'll even offer you a boon. Use it as you see fit. When you're done, *bring me his soul*."

Danni's eye flicked to the dissipating cloud and the man she barely knew. What did the Baron want with him? Was she even within her purview to ask?

"*Non*. It isn't," The Baron chided her. "But I shall sweeten the pot for you. Do as I ask…"

His hand traveled from her chin to her chest, where he stopped to set a finger against the metal secreted beneath her skin.

"…And you can truly be done with me."

Danni narrowed her eyes. The devil was in the details, and none more fiendish that the one staring at her now.

"Say it," she said.

"I will pluck out my nail." He drew a smoldering X over his heart. "My word."

Her own hand came up to touch the hard head of the coffin nail buried in her breastbone. "His soul for my freedom?"

He nodded once.

"And if I refuse?" she asked.

The Baron laughed a self-satisfied chuckle and flicked his wrist in the air, making a little flourish with his fingertips. His eyes blazed with raw power.

"You can join me now."

The island where they stood began to rumble as something moved beneath it. The swamp shimmered and split in a wave that rose but never crested. It hummed with incandescent energy as a thousand faces screamed up and out. Their expressions blended together, anger and grief, each one as indistinct as the last.

The Crossroads.

Danni squared her shoulders. "Deal."

The Baron closed the gap between them and laid his mouth against hers. His kiss was like the air of an open grave, dank and stinking of mud. Their agreement seared into her lips, across her tongue, and burned inside her mouth.

The Baron withdrew and smiled. "*Bon chance.*"

The yellow-eyed snake was back at her breast, his sinewy head craned out and poised to strike. A whimper escaped her lips.

A second later, it struck true.

Five

Danni's eyes snapped open on an unfamiliar face inches from her own.

"Whoa, wait! You're safe. You're at Mount Carmel convent. I'm Sister Levine."

The sister stepped back slowly to allow Danni to sit upright.

Danni's skin felt stiff and sticky. She palmed her face and chest, but only found the sweat-damped sundress. In the soft light of the bedside lamp, she could see the dirt worn into the fabric. The whole thing past recovery, and well past needing a wash.

"Any pain?" Sister Levine reached for Danni's wrist and set two cool fingers against her pulse.

Danni pulled back, gripped her own wrist, and stared at the dry gauze wound around her hand. "No. Yes. What the hell happened to my hand?"

"Michael said when you lost consciousness you fell onto some glass."

Michael.

Danni's voice came out in a low growl. "Where is he?"

Sister Levine's stayed polite. "He had to run an errand. If there's anything you need, I'll be happy to get it. But first…"

She tucked the edge of her skirt around her legs and sat beside Danni on the bed. "Do want to tell me what happened to you?"

"Not really." The sister gave her a withering look and Danni sighed. "I… fainted. Sort of."

"*Sort of*," Sister Levine repeated. She pulled the stethoscope from her neck. "Does that happen often?"

However lighthearted she'd meant for it to sound, it was a stupid question and deserved an equally stupid answer. Rather than give one, Danni leaned back against the headboard and crossed her arms.

"What I mean to say is," Sister Levine continued, "if there's something you need to stop… whatever this is… from happening again, I can get it for you."

No. She really couldn't. Danni shrugged.

Finally, Sister Levine stood and gathered a medical bag from beside the bed then gestured toward a narrow door.

"You can shower in there. I'll have fresh clothes for you when you're done."

When she reached the door, she stopped, as if she wanted to say something more, then simply pulled it closed behind her.

Danni stood. Her fingers brushed the ceiling as she arched upward to work all the kinks from her spine. Bed. Table. Chair. Four walls and a slim window on the west wall. The word 'cell' came to mind. It was less than four steps from the wall to the center of the room. Three more to the bathroom. At least the shower felt good.

She worked a quick lather into her hair, scrubbing out the last bits of sweat and grit. Water swirled pink around the drain at her feet. She unwound the long string of gauze and let it fall into the basin.

The cut wasn't bad, deep but clean. She gathered a wad of spit in her mouth and hacked it into her palm. It sat there for a minute, shimmering like the inside of a clamshell held out to the sun. Slowly, the wound stitched itself closed. The angry red line grew duller and duller until all that remained was the smooth pink pad of her hand.

The shower knobs made a shrill screech as she twisted them off. She shook the water out of her hair. When she unfolded the curtain, a thick white towel sat within arm's reach. It hadn't been there when she got in, and it unnerved her to think someone had been so close and she'd never heard them.

The towel swallowed her neck to knee and smelled like lavender and lye. As promised, fresh clothes had been laid out neatly across the bed, but she heaved a weary sigh when she saw them.

The white dress shirt would do, as would the black vest, but the knee-highs and the pleated tartan skirt were out of the question. She scanned the room. Her dress was gone, leaving her no other option. Grudgingly, she tugged the skirt up over her hips and twisted this way and that, then tried several times to find a comfortable way to sit.

Three cautious knocks pulled her attention to the door. She chucked the knee-highs on the floor with the damp towel and gave the skirt a few more tugs.

"Come in."

Michael stepped through the door then pressed his back against it until it latched.

"How do you feel?" he asked.

"Kind of like I should be in detention. Any chance of getting my own clothes back?"

"Maybe after penance." He grinned but it didn't reach the concern in his eyes. "What happened to you? You collapsed … I didn't know … has that happened before?" he asked.

"Twice today, by my count. First time was your fault."

"Fair enough, but the second?"

She ran her hands through her damp hair, sighed, but didn't answer.

"Do I owe these sisters something?"

"Not money, certainly. But if you feel like you owe them something, that might help."

"I don't *feel* anything, but I won't skip on a tab."

Danni scanned his face. He was on the high side of his thirties, or maybe he'd just had that rough of a life. If he was native to New Orleans, he would have aged double just in the last few years alone. Katrina had done that to people, left creases in their expression as telltale as the watermarks on their homes.

"Where were you?" she asked. "For the storm?"

"Here."

Michael stepped forward.

"Did you know that the sisters, almost all of them, stayed in New Orleans through Katrina, too? They gave shelter and food to thousands of injured and stranded people. The second floor balcony was a boat dock for awhile.

"These old girls are tough. They don't shake easy. But right now … well, let's just say they're concerned."

"About what?" she asked.

"Something dark moving around in the Ninth, snatching up nuns."

"Is it possible they just decided to take a vacation?" she suggested, somewhat half-heartedly.

The proud smile climbed back into his face. "They don't know the meaning of the word.

"But it's not just the sisters who've gone missing. Other people are, too. Some of them children."

"How many are we talking here?"

"It's… kind of hard to say. Five sisters. A dozen others maybe. I've heard tell of shadow men, gangs. One guy told me he saw the red horseman of the Apocalypse."

"Pestilence?"

"War," he corrected. "Or mass slaughter, depending on your version of the Bible."

Danni frowned. "I see."

She sat back on the bed. She could think of a hundred dark places, and a hundred darker things someone might want with a few terrified women. Still, the sisters weren't exactly easy prey.

Michael's story fell a little short of how tough these 'old birds' really were. Danni had also been in New Orleans for the storm and remembered what some called the 'indomitable will' of the Sisters of Mt. Carmel. In the post Katrina days, when chaos for chaos' sake had driven gangs out to free roam the streets, 'standing your ground' was less about faith and more about having twelve in the clip and one in the barrel. It had been something out of an action movie: nuns with sawed-offs. But there had been no cameras rolling. It was as real as it was terrifying.

"And you think I'm going to be able to find … whatever this is?"

"I certainly hope so."

"Why?" she asked.

"I'll show you, if you'd like."

She pointed a hard finger at him. "I haven't agreed to anything yet."

He stepped forward again and squatted down so they were eye to eye. "If the sisters don't have anything you want, tell me who does. I'll find them. Whatever it is, whatever I have to do."

Maybe it was the boldness of it, or the underlying desperation in his voice. She crossed her arms, bowed her head, and tried to think.

The Baron was the scariest thing she knew. If not him, who would want a bunch of nuns? Her thoughts drifted farther. What *did* the Baron want? Her eyes opened on Michael.

His voice softened to almost a whisper. "Please, tell me what you're thinking."

"I'm trying to imagine what someone could do with a bunch of nuns," she said finally. "It's not like you just send a ransom note to the Vatican. And …"

"And?" he pressed.

She swallowed, looked up, and held his gaze. "This *is* New Orleans."

He visibly flinched and tore his face away from hers, fixing his eyes to a spot on the floor. The whisper was still in his voice, but it was edged with ice.

"I can't afford to …" He paused and shook his head. "I *won't* think like that."

Danni laid a finger against the edge of his jaw and guided his eyes back to hers. Where she'd expected to find anger, she only saw dread. It drew thin lines around his temples as his jaw tightened.

"But I can," she said.

His voice was rasped when he spoke again. "Are you saying you'll help me?"

She nodded once.

"And in return?" he asked.

"You'll owe me."

A hand slid out from her lap again, fingers wiggling in the air between them. "Deal?"

If he hesitated, Danni couldn't perceive it. She was focused on his hand closing around hers, or more importantly, her index finger where it brushed against his pulse.

The sensation was instant. His heartbeat moved in concert with his soul, as blinding and real as it had been on the boat, but with no images attached. The longer she looked, the less she saw, the more frustrating it became. Finally, she withdrew her hand from his.

First things first. If she was going to satisfy the Baron and earn her freedom, she was going to need her knife back.

Six

"And how's your charge?" Mother Superior asked.

Michael grimaced. "She isn't my charge, Mother. She's her own person. But she's agreed to help, and we need her."

The half-light of a desk lamp met the glare of a flat screen monitor and cast a dim shadow on a century-old wooden chair. The shadow in it rolled closer to the desk and became the slight figure of an elderly woman studying him. "Perhaps."

"You're not sure?"

"Frankly, no." The eyes behind her banker's glasses were sharp and clear. "I trust you, Michael. That doesn't mean I'm going to trust her. And I'm not sure you should."

"Me either," he admitted. "But I believe she is more than her failings, more than her sins." He grinned at her. "Aren't we all?"

"Pride is still a sin, boy."

"Faith isn't."

"Depends on where it's placed."

Michael sat on the edge of the chair just beyond her desk.

"You believe that God sent you to New Orleans, right?" he asked. "Is it so hard to believe that he would send you some help?"

Mother Superior nodded once. "He sent me you."

"Yeah, well, now he's sending me some."

"At what cost?"

"I'll owe her a favor, like tickets to a Saints game."

Her gaze turned to steel. "Probably something more serious than that."

He stood again and leaned over the desk. The pulse in his hands beat against the aged wood.

"I have to find them, Mother. I have to protect the rest. I have to try."

She met his gaze, waiting. Watching. Off in the distance, the St. Louis Cathedral bells chimed the hour.

Mother Superior turned back to her keyboard. "You'd best be off, then. And stop calling me Mother. It's cheeky. God go with you, boy."

Stained-glass sconces threw yellowish light down the walls while late June bugs banged themselves against the glass. The hallway was silent except for a few box fans pushing around hot air.

Danni moved soundlessly toward the stairs. She took the first two steps quickly but froze when the third creaked under her foot. The sound echoed through the stairwell, amplified by the hush. She listened for a long minute before working her way down to the first floor as quickly as she could.

The clock in the common room read just past midnight. Danni stopped at the kitchen pass-through. She tried the door, but it was locked. She needed fresh air.

She wandered past the uneasy eyes of painted saints and checked a few more doors. They were all locked with double-keyed, iron deadbolts. A lot of security for a few nuns.

Finally, she found one that led her into a garden cloister lit by tall, amber street lamps. A fountain babbled in the center, washing water down a loose pile of slick, flat rocks.

"May I help you?"

Danni jumped and swallowed a startled yelp. A wisp of a woman appeared out of the shadows. Her eyes were strong, solid, and exacting as they looked Danni up and down.

"You scared me," Danni said.

"Did I? I wouldn't suppose *you* would frighten so easily."

"Oh, great," Danni said under her breath.

"Do you know who I am?"

"A nun?"

"Mother Superior."

Danni shrugged. "The head nun, then. Should I curtsy?"

"Have a seat, Danielle."

Mother Superior gestured toward a sandstone bench and tapped the edge of a file folder against her palm. She tossed it to land at Danni's feet with a sharp smack. Danni stared at it and then leaned back and crossed her arms.

Mother Superior shrugged. "The police chief is a friend."

"Don't you mean a congregant?"

"That, too." Mother Superior smiled for a moment but, it faded quickly as she pointed at the folder.

"Quite a history you have. Grand larceny, burglary, possession of stolen property …"

"I served my time."

"Yes, I'm sure three years in Ducane Women's Correctional Facility provided ample time to perfect your skills."

"The warden a *friend* of yours, too?"

Mother Superior face stayed an implacable mask.

Danni blew a long breath through her nose. "I thought nuns were all about forgiveness. Hate the sin, love the sinner. All that stuff."

"I *do* love you, Danielle. You are a child of God. Same as the rest of us. It's the other gods you consort with that scare me."

At that, Danni had to chuckle. "Huh. Wouldn't think you'd frighten so easily."

Mother Superior smiled.

"Fear can be a useful tool. In this case, it gave me the caution to weigh Michael's suggestion carefully." She pointed to the file folder. "I need to know who you are to understand if we really need you."

Danni smoothed the skirt back down over her thighs as she stood. "And? Who am I, Sister?"

Mother Superior considered her for a long moment.

"That you would ask makes me wonder if even you know."

Finally, she asked, "*Will* you help?"

"I told Michael I would."

Mother Superior nodded. "Then go with God."

She crossed the garden and held open the door. Danni let out a long breath and started after her.

"Do you always get this personal with the help?"

The old nun chuckled. "When it means protecting my own? You bet your ass."

Seven

The Baron had a flare for the dramatic, she'd give him that.

Danni's eyes had only just closed on the sparse surroundings of the convent, so the banquet hall she opened them on seemed that much more garish by design. A long, dark table with massive claw-foot legs spanned the length of the room. The royal purple runner down the center was covered in fruits, roasted meats, and some delicacies she couldn't immediately name. Duck confit, she recognized that.

Iron candelabras held pillars of earth-tone candles. Wax spilled down the length of each of them before falling into pools against the stone floor.

Maybe it was because she had seen him so recently, but the Baron seemed much less impressive in the center of it all. His white top hat was trimmed with pheasant feathers and roses, giving him a Victorian appearance as he sat back in the chair at the far end of the table.

"You're underdressed, *cher*."

She was still wearing the tartan patterned skirt and

dress shirt, making her question how much of this world she actually controlled. She suspected it was a blend of her conscious mind and the Baron's influence. If so, it made sense that she would appear in the last thing she recalled wearing.

She stepped away from the table with a sigh and spread her arms out at her sides.

"Then dress me, Mr. Darcy."

The Baron frowned. "I'm afraid I don't know the reference."

"*Pride and Prejudice?*" He shook his head. Danni shrugged.

"You're what, a couple hundred years old? I would have assumed you would have gotten around to reading it."

"Couple *thousand*," he growled. "And I have no interest in the folly of mortal men."

"Seems like that's all you have an interest in," she muttered.

The Baron hesitated a moment longer. He held a gloved hand in the air beside his head. The leather creaked as he dusted his fingertips together and then snapped.

The weight of her clothes faded, only to be replaced with a stiffer material. When she looked down, she was unsurprised to see a deep blue, period dress that accentuated her chest but flared wide around her feet. The underlying crinoline itched around her ankles, and the bodice felt like it had been cinched a full turn tighter than was ever meant to be comfortable. But it was better than snakes.

"Serve me," the Baron instructed.

Danni snagged a large silver bowl full of fat, red-bodied crawfish and marched down the table. She tossed a few on his empty plate with her bare hands. They slid over the edge and into his lap. She dropped the bowl beside him and curtsied.

"M'lord," she sneered.

The Baron's hand shot out and seized her throat, locking out her breath.

"You'd do well you remember that!"

Danni gasped, trying hard to ignore the stench of burnt sugar as it poured off of him in heated waves. She wrapped her hand around his wrist, trying and failing to break his grip. Her vision began to spot and darken. Was she choking in the waking world? Or was it all just her mind imagining what she would feel if he were actually touching her? A thought struck her. Why would she need to breathe in a dream?

All at once, her vision returned. The pain of his hand faded to a mere presence. The Baron withdrew but said nothing as he went about picking the crawfish from his lap and tossing them onto the plate.

"You can't hurt me here," she said, more a startled observation than a question.

"I *can* hurt you," he corrected quickly. "But only in the ways you think you should be hurt. Well discovered, *cher*. Took you long enough."

He pinched the head of a crawfish and sucked hard on the tail. It made a wet noise around the edge of his lips.

"How goes your quarry?"

Danni withdrew the chair beside him and sat stiffly.

"A little help would be nice. What makes him so special? Why can't I see his soul?"

The Baron lifted his chin as if he was listening to something she could not hear. After a minute, he looked at her again, pressed his thumb and index fingers together, and ran them over his lips.

Danni sighed. "Okay. Well, if you won't tell me that…
what's going on in the Ninth Ward?"

Again, the Baron seemed to consider the air before
answering. This time, he nodded.

"The question is what are you willing to trade for that
information, *cher*?"

She groaned inwardly. "What do you want?"

The Baron tossed the shell against his plate and then sat
back. Danni watched in silence as he slowly tugged off the
tip of each gloved finger, removing them with cultured
precision. When he finished, he pointed to a whole peach
resting on the top of the centerpiece. Danni took a deep
breath before standing to retrieve it.

He motioned her around in front of him. A single,
bladed nail slid around the flesh of the peach. The Baron
twisted it into two halves, tossing one on the table behind
her before biting out the heart of the other.

"Things have not always been adversarial between us."

As if to make the point, he extended his juice-soaked
fingers.

"The Ninth?" she asked again.

"Is in need of an exterminator."

Against his accent, the word had one too many
syllables.

"What kind of exterminator?"

"Ah, ah, *cher*. Tit for tat."

Danni grasped his wrist with both hands and drew his
fingers into her mouth. They tasted sweet at first. But the
longer it lasted, the more she could taste the spice in his
skin. She withdrew slowly, but held his eyes. A breath
shuddered from between his lips.

"What kind of exterminator?" she repeated.

"The kind who specializes in snakes."

It *always* had to be snakes.

His hands found the stays at the top of her bust, but instead of working the laces open he ran a burning finger down the center of the corset. The fabric hissed and split, leaving only the thin, cotton chemise against her skin. When he reached for her again, she pulled away.

"Tell me how."

Instead of a direct answer, The Baron began to sing. "My pahrain and your pahrain were sittin' on the bayou…"

With each line he advanced until his chest was against hers. He used his body weight to press her backwards against the table. At what point the food had disappeared and it had become a bed, she couldn't say. The Baron darted forward and kissed her, quick but wet, then continued to move across her body. His lips left wakes of goosebumps across her skin.

"And the nuns?" she asked.

He returned to eye level with her again, but his hand stayed moving beneath the layers of skirt.

"Shall I go on?" he asked.

Danni closed her eyes and let her thoughts drift. She could feel the internal tension of her mind reflected in her waking body, but it was shifting with every quick kiss the Baron laid across her lips and over her jaw. She could feel his smile against her throat.

"Shall I go on, *cher*?" he asked again as if he already knew the answer.

Danni nodded dully before succumbing fully to his touch. His voice fell hot against her ear.

"The nuns are dead."

Eight

When morning crept over New Orleans, the sky was
full of dark clouds and the air with the scent of wet
pavement. Michael found Danni at a table in the convent's
common room, coffee in one hand and her head in the
other.

"Coffee looks good. You, not so much," he said.
"Couldn't sleep?"

She pushed the hair back from her face and sniffed a
laugh.

"Too quiet," she said.

He pulled a cup off a sideboard and sat opposite her. He
mechanically dumped six spoonfuls of sugar into the cup,
added a bare drop of milk after it, and reached for the
coffee pot to cover the evidence.

"You're a city sleeper, aren't you? Like all the
background noise, the cars, the jazz?"

It was true, but she hadn't noticed its absence until last
night when the eerie quiet of the convent had forced her
attention inward, grinding it down to a single point. Then,
when she *had* fallen asleep...

She shoved the thought away and let her eyes wander over the common room. The nuns moved silently between the long, communal tables. They shot wary glances in her direction and murmured what she could only assume was quiet displeasure at her presence.

How did she begin to tell them their sisters were dead?

"You haven't heard a thing I've said, have you?" Michael said.

Her mind pulled back, and she held an open-mouthed gape for a long moment. How did she tell Michael?

"No, I'm sorry. I was—"

"Lost in thought. I noticed." He tipped the cup back and drank it in one long swallow. "You ready? I have a few things I need to show you."

"I need to stop by my place for a pair of jeans." She smoothed the tartan cloth over her hip. "I'm tired of crossing my ankles."

"Sure thing. Let's go."

Outside, sunlight poked through the clouds and bit her bleary eyes. She lifted her hand to her forehead and followed Michael's shadow across the grass to a primer brown and gray pick-up at the end of the parking lot. Michael went around to the passenger side and held the door open for her. She was pretty sure she could walk faster.

"You're serious with this shit?" she asked.

"Absolutely. If we lose it, I don't want to care."

He waited until she was in and then closed the door. It took a few tries. He had to reach through the open window for the driver's side handle, but once he was settled, the old truck started on the first turn.

"Sorry, no seat belts," he said.

"I think that's the least of our problems."

The shocks were either soft or missing, so the cab swayed side to side as it climbed through every intersection. She gave him quick directions to her apartment and sat back to watch him from her periphery.

His green eyes glinted in the new day's sun. Paired with the damp swoop of red hair, he had a slightly ethereal look. Showered and shaved, the deeper tension had faded from his skin, to leave it smooth and lineless.

"Are you originally from New Orleans?" she asked.

"You're not." He smiled but kept his eyes on the road. "You don't say it right. It's *N'awlins*, and yeah. I am."

"Have you always lived at the convent?"

He looked surprised for a moment.

"I assumed," she said. "Since you didn't offer to take me home last night."

In truth, he hadn't even considered it, but it stalled his speech for a full minute.

"You stayed anyway," he said eventually.

For that, Danni had no answer.

He made a sharp turn off Canal Street. She smelled smoke and the acrid tang of burning plaster and insulation. Less than a block away, black clouds roiled and spread against the white sky. Michael steered the truck to the curb.

"Tell me that's not your building," he said.

"Afraid so."

Her finger guided his attention to the second floor where her curtains were spread out in the updraft. Sirens screamed in the distance, but they were racing toward a lost cause. Fire swept out of every window and into the eaves.

Danni slipped from the passenger's seat and cocked a hip against the truck bed. The once-red brick was now a hunk of crumbling black, charred from the inside and out. Her eyes worked over it, trying to find a source, a place that burned brighter than the rest. The heat grew thicker and made it hard to breathe. Across the street, neighbors she knew only by face stood in a cluster of consoling arms, moving with the passive exhaustion of hurricane survivors. Hell, most of them were. Most of them had nothing already. Now they had less of it.

A couple of teenagers broke from the pack and took a few steps before laying down skateboards. She flagged down the boy from the apartment below hers. He caught the lamppost and turned a full three-sixty before skidding to a stop.

"You see what happened?" she asked.

He shook his head. "Ma says that pair of tweekers in the basement probably knocked over a coffee can or somethin'."

"Anyone seen them?"

"Nah. Prolly still in there."

He pushed himself around the pole and off down the street.

Michael's voice and his firm hand on her shoulder jerked her around again.

"I am so sorry."

She shrugged. "It is what it is. And it wasn't much. Bed, some clothes. I'll miss that shower though."

The first wave of fire trucks pulled onto the street. Two hydrants opened with a clanging hiss. The first wave of water exploded from the nozzle and clouded to white steam as it met the rising heat. Water rained down, soaking bystanders as the firemen trained their hoses on the building in a feeble attempt to stop the spread.

More sirens yipped up between buildings, and a tight group of police cars sluiced through the run-off already rushing toward the sewer grates.

Danni thumped a knuckle against Michael's chest.

"Let's go before you're blocked in."

"Don't you want to … " He pointed to the hustle of bodies behind him.

"Not even remotely. Come on."

She settled back in the truck. Michael stayed outside and made a quick call. Her eyes flicked between the cellphone, the burning building, and the growing number of cops herding the newly-homeless back to a safe distance.

A minute later, the driver's door opened with an iron groan and slammed even uglier. Michael popped the clutch and let gravity carry them back a few feet before making a wide turn back into traffic.

"You sure you're okay?" he asked after a minute.

"I'm fine. It wasn't the meth heads, though. I chased them out weeks ago."

He started to ask the obvious question and then thought better of it.

"I'm guessing you don't have renter's insurance, huh?"

She frowned at him. "I don't even have a lease."

If he was waiting for explanation, she didn't offer one. He cruised through two more intersections before speaking again.

"Well, you're still going to need some clothes, and you don't look like a big box store kind of girl to me. So…"

He eased the truck up to the curb and gestured to a storefront. "Welcome to Nouveau Victoria's."

She leaned toward his window and narrowed her eyes on big, red letters monogrammed on the glass doors.

"Looks closed to me."

Michael pulled a single key from his pocket.

"Victoria said to take your pick of the lot. 'Course, she also said it was on me, so go gentle, okay?"

She followed him to the sidewalk. He slid the key into the lock then reached in to flip the lights. The store lit up from the inside, but Danni remained planted at the curb.

"You want me to walk into a store and fill a bag?" she asked.

"Well ... yeah." Michael tipped his head. "Something wrong with that?"

"Some people call that theft."

"All the cops are across town at your place."

He chuckled, but sobered quickly when he realized he was the only one laughing.

"Victoria said it's fine. Come on."

When he reached for her, she recoiled. He searched her face for explanation before coming up with his own.

"Wouldn't take a free lunch if you were starving, would you?"

Her eyes narrowed. "Nothing is ever *free*."

She eased past him and into the store but kept her arms crossed as she surveyed the racks of clothing. Someone had gone to a lot of work picking patterns that managed to be both regional and fashionable, which, in New Orleans, meant a collection of greens and lavenders, sequins and gold lamé. Still, it wasn't all bad. She flipped through a short stack of t-shirts in bold primary colors.

"The proprietor a *friend* of yours?" she asked.

"Not the way you mean it, I'm sure."

Michael grabbed a leather duffel bag off the top of a rack and tossed it against her chest, but the humor was gone from his voice.

"I wasn't kidding. Get what you need."

She stuffed a few t-shirts into the bag before tossing it back, equally hard. "Satisfied?"

He frowned and wagged a finger at her skirt. "I thought

you wanted to get rid of that?"

The thin zipper at the back of the skirt gave way with a little tug and she let it fall around her ankles. Michael twisted his head to stare at the far wall. She hooked it with her toe and kicked it into his face. He jerked it away in time to see her sashay past him to a rack of jeans.

She stabbed her feet through the legs while Michael grabbed two more pairs of jeans and a handful of shirts. He dropped the bag on the floor between them and retreated to an old, bench-style window seat.

"Intimates are that way." He sat down and scrubbed his face with his hand, suddenly tired. "Really. I mean it. Get what you need, whatever you need. We might not get a chance to do this again."

Hunched over his knees, he looked more anxious than aggravated, more careworn than anything, and he seemed to be muttering something under his breath. She nodded, but gave him a second look before passing through the sheer curtain dividing the room.

There was a fine line between what he called 'intimates' and what Victoria was selling. It took a minute of shuffling through racks of crotch-less panties to find some with, well…

She stuffed a handful of things in the bag, not really paying attention, not really believing it mattered, and then stared dimly into the bundle of cloth in the bag. It was now *everything* she owned.

As she passed through the curtain again, her eyes flashed over a carnelian cocktail dress centered on the wall. While the red satin covered neck to mid-thigh, the back mirrored the front in negative space. Her fingers traced the cool fabric.

"If you like it, get it," he said softly.

She turned the price tag over in her fingers before releasing a long, low whistle.

"It's a little expensive for my taste."

He started to protest, but she stopped him with a quick wave of the bag. "This will do."

"Almost."

He dropped a pair of black motorcycle boots in front of her.

Danni pulled them over her feet and cinched the laces down tight before making a slow pirouette.

"Good?" she asked.

He shrugged. "They'd look better with the skirt."

Nine

Michael drove east to the I-10 and then switched to the 510 just long enough to catch the next exit. It ended abruptly with a roadblock. Michael jammed the brakes and yanked the truck off onto an overgrown pathway. Small scrub oaks and willow limbs bounced off the windshield as he fought to keep the truck on the rutted path.

Danni levered herself up in the seat for a cleaner view. The dark shell of a Ferris wheel towered in the distance. Broken spokes hung away from its body, making it look like a hand trying to pull the sky down on top of it.

"Did you ever come here," Michael asked. "Back before the storm?"

Danni screwed up her face. "An amusement park? Sweaty strangers and small kids screaming in a heat wave?"

"Aw, come on. It's Bluesland. Pick up bands and carnies on a boardwalk, *étouffée* and hot licks in the air …"

"Cheesy, plastic trinkets and pushy tourists packed in like cattle."

"It wasn't *that* bad," Michael protested.

"Yes, it was. The only reason any local would come here was looking for easy marks. And the work wasn't worth the return." She flashed him a snide smile. "Better options elsewhere, you know?"

Clearly, he didn't.

"Yeah, I guess," he said. "But the coasters were great. At least until Katrina put the whole place underwater."

Michael parked against a stand of trees and killed the engine.

"We're on foot from here."

When she stepped from the truck, the tension in her spine fed down into her gut. She'd been to Bluesland, once. When she followed him to the mouth of the path that led deeper into the park, she felt the dread wash over her again.

"Michael, what are we doing here?"

"Something I want you to see."

He led her through the clearing and along a dirt and gravel path. Rusted, ragged chain link marked the point where a gate used to stand. A faded shape was burned into the asphalt at the entrance. It looked like a simple A-frame tent with the ground lines stretching off to the edge of the asphalt on each side. He stopped and pressed his fingers into the metal, clearing away the dirt to expose the marking underneath.

"That's a *veve*," Michael said.

"Yeah."

"A warning *veve*."

Danni gritted her teeth. "*I know.*"

Michael stumbled over a fence post bent parallel to the ground. They weaved around the twisted remains of a refreshment stand and piles of corrugated metal, ripped and rusting in the sun. The pavement opened to a clearing of faded, wooden picnic tables. Danni kicked one. When it didn't give, she sat. Michael stopped, seeming confused.

"Last time I'll ask," she said. "What are we doing here?"

"You said you wanted to know how I found you." He waved his hand toward the path. "Easier to just show you."

There was nothing here she hadn't seen, only things she'd successfully forgotten and wasn't looking to recall.

Michael waited, watched, and then after a minute said, "You don't want to be here."

"I'm not *comfortable* being here," Danni corrected. "And you really shouldn't be either."

He pushed himself away from the pole and reached deep into his back pocket. When he extended his arm again, her knife was held between his thumb and forefinger. "This make you feel better?"

She didn't reach for it immediately. "I thought you dropped that in the Mississippi."

He turned it over in his fist and then swept his fingers closed around it. When he opened his hand, it was gone. He closed his fist again and it was back. He repeated the trick a few times, letting her follow the motion, and shrugged.

"Street magician taught me how to do that when I was ten. Considering you were out of it at the time, probably looked just like that."

She shoved herself off the table and sneered. "Cute trick."

"It got me some street money, now and then."

"Yeah? Bet I got more like this."

She grabbed his arm and wrenched the knife away, then slammed his hand down against the picnic table. He flinched as the blade flashed down, but she held him in place as the tip drove into the soft wood. She sent a series of rapid stabs into the narrow spaces between each of his fingers, working her way thumb to pinky and back. She saw his eyes widen when he realized she wasn't even looking at his hand.

Her lips moved close enough for her breath to heat his ear. "*My* knife. Not yours."

She released his wrist and flipped the blade in the air before pocketing it.

"Your knife." He wrung his hands together, flexing his fingers. "What does it do anyway?"

"Cuts things."

Fifty yards farther on, the cracked pavement led off in two directions. Michael pointed to the right. Danni stayed with him as they moved through a corral of empty game stalls. A few water-soaked teddy bears hung in defeat from the painted backdrops of ring tosses and bulls-eyes. Where the stalls ended, Michael ducked under an enormous metal tube.

"Look at this," Michael said. "Used to be part of a water slide. That's gotta be twelve feet around. Must weigh tons. Can you imagine the force it took to rip it free?"

Imagine? She shot him a sideways glance, opened her mouth and then resigned herself to shrug.

Ahead, a large paneled building sat in the center of the park. She could make out the faded figures in the advertisements painted on it. Garish lettering that once had shouted to fun-seekers now whispered of adventure.

"Michael—"

"Almost there. Promise," he said.

He guided her around the corner, out of sight from the sidewalk and to an octagonal structure. The wooden walls stood fifteen feet on a side, but had no windows.

"Probably put the walls up to protect the ride," Michael

said. "Not that it did much good."

The walls were covered in color, bold spray-painted letters in purple and green, red and yellow. Some were bold and blocky, two or three feet high, while others were delicate lines that blended into abstract scenes. The faded figures of dancing metal horses now sat on a backdrop for an artist's urgent madness.

"The carousel," Danni whispered.

"Yeah," Michael said. "I used to love this thing. The sisters and I brought children here, and I'd ride with the young ones and the whole park spun around us. Show's on the inside these days."

The plywood door creaked open on one rusty hinge as Michael pushed it back.

"Hold it open for a minute so I can see."

Danni caught the edge of the swollen door. He reached down to the floor inside to pull out an old paint can secreted inside the door's shadow. He produced a lighter and lit the rag in the can.

"Sure that thing won't blow up?" she asked.

"Nope."

Michael felt around the inside walls, using the first can to set small fires in others around the octagon. The torches gave off a dull glow, illuminating the letters scrawled up and down the inside walls.

"Best I can tell, it's some kind of message center."

He ran a lazy hand over the walls, across prayers, phone numbers, and pleas for any information about the missing. She'd seen others around the Quarter, but mostly where the foot traffic was heavy. This one seemed pointless.

"Here." Michael pressed a finger against a name. "Christopher Maurice Durant. I know him. Well, knew him. He used to go to the convent school."

"Looks like whoever put this here knew that, too," Danni said.

Though the name had been written in fat permanent marker, the cross that covered it had been gouged a good quarter inch into the plywood. The wood was still splintered white and raw, which meant it was a recent addition. There were more farther down the wall. Names that had been crossed out. Were they all dead? She counted a dozen. Why leave them here? Halfway around the room, Danni stopped.

"I know this pattern."

She worked her nail under a different carved edge in the wood. Two caskets set on either side of an altered cross, and below that, a compass circle drawn out in four directions.

"The Crossroads."

Michael's nod was grave, and he pointed farther down the wall to a charcoal drawing of a skeleton in top hat and tails, his cane in one hand as the other extended farther around the circle. They followed it and came to another. In this one, the skeleton was holding a series of playing cards, all aces and one black king, the king being the spitting image of the skeleton himself. Next to that, the skeleton king was seated on a throne of bleach-white bone.

"Seems about right," Danni muttered.

In the last one, his resting hand was open and palming a tiny, drawn carousel. It was brilliant against the black and white of his hand. Blazing crimsons, greens and purples danced out from its center. Danni sucked in a quick breath and cast a wary glance at the dark, full-sized carousel behind them.

Michael motioned her onto the rusty platform and pointed to an open spot next to a faded unicorn before disappearing into the center hub of the carousel.

The room lit up around Danni as Michael reappeared from behind a small door in the hub.

"It's a barrel fire set into the center where the lights used to be," he said. "But it won't last long."

He grabbed one of the support poles and leaned his shoulder against it. The carousel shuddered but didn't move.

"You think you're gonna *push* this thing around?"

"Not…far," he grunted. "There's a…gas motor… in there, I just need… to get… it going!"

The platform began to turn, the whole thing protesting the weight of its own force as it finished the first revolution. The second time around, a gear chunked and the motor came to life. The carousel began to move under its own power.

The first few circuits were slow. Danni braced a hand on the patina stock pierced through the unicorn. His face had melted and his eyes were swells of brown, curdled plastic. He shared the platform with a mermaid who'd definitely seen better days, half a griffin, and a headless swan that now swung free of its anchor and struck the rails with a hollow *ka-tunk*.

As the carousel picked up speed, the graffiti lost all context, colors blended by motion as the light at the center burst with an audible crackle. Danni flinched and raised a hand to shield her eyes from the glaring light. White flares ribboned out through the slotted pillars and split the stamped-steel floor with hard, medial lines. The increasing spin threw her perception, and she lost sight of Michael as well as a clear position on the door. Each revolution pitched her faster, pinning her with the centrifugal force of a few tons of oxidized steel.

Cooler, moving air lifted her hair off her neck while the entire thing continued to spin with far greater force than it ought to. She wrenched herself forward, taking one leaden step after another toward the edge of the platform. A clean tuck and roll was probably the only safe way off.

Then she saw it. The variegated graffiti, streaking by with no certain form, began to expand into bolder patterns. But just as they would begin to hold their shape they'd collapse again, like a stutter-start on a cold engine.

Deeper inside the carousel, she heard the mechanized whine of gears grinding out a final pulse of speed. At what seemed like full acceleration, the entire thing shuddered and bolts unseated under the strain. Danni clung to the loosening supports and fixed her eyes to the rapid fusion of color and light on the wall.

A crowd of faces took shape, men and women, crude in composition but colored by unmistakable rage. They shook weapons above their heads. They swarmed and collapsed across the ground, spilling over the bright background of Bluesland with ravenous speed. Children screamed and ran beneath them, desperate to avoid the onslaught of hungry, desperate souls consuming the stragglers that fell from the herd. The world fell to ruin in their wake, and the color drained from the shadows.

The ground broke, bringing up a colder, bluer light. The angry mob roared, unwilling to be tamed. The ground split wider. Another cloud rose to meet them, a faceless silhouette fashioned out of cardinal red. It swelled and collided with the mob. Blood-lusting laughter morphed into horrified screams. Bodies pulled apart in all directions, twisting down through the open earth. The mass of voices fell away one by one.

The red cloud stood alone. Children laughed again and

the sound brought smaller shapes into view. Arms reached out to grasp, hold. Red hands reached back, brushing broader palms against them. The red form began to lighten, crimson to pink to dusky peach, features shading down to form sharper, harder lines. A lithe, shapely body. Black hair. White skin. Danni was watching herself.

And somewhere deep in the swamp around Bluesland, the Baron Samedi was laughing.

The piercing screech of moving metal gave Danni no time to brace for impact. Instead of the calm deceleration she'd hoped for, the entire carousel shuddered and then seized. Her hands tore from the pole as her body continued through the final spin, out and away, and into the painted wall.

She landed hard and stayed there, counting off the seconds between breaths before testing the muscles for injury. She spat grit, water mold. Michael ran to her.

"Are you alright?"

She caught the hand he held out to her.

"Oh, yeah. Right as rain," she groaned.

She scrubbed her fingers against the wall and sniffed the crusted paint. Plaster dust and cooking grease, a smell that pitched her stomach forward and back. Bile burned at the back of her throat, and she swallowed the rising rage. She held a tight fist against her mouth and closed her eyes, but only saw the painted image of herself in a throbbing, red darkness. She fled from the carousel stall in search of something familiar and alive.

The images, the things she had done, chased her. She bent over her knees and let her stomach empty a dark coffee-scented pool at her feet. She retched a few more times before pulling upright again and wiping her mouth with the back of her hand.

Michael reached for her but stopped when she waved him off.

"*How* did you find that?" she asked.

"Joto knew about it. About you. Rumors mostly, but look, I wasn't lying. I do odd jobs for the sisters. When someone is causing them trouble, I help out. But whatever is happening in the Ninth … " He pointed back to the carousel. "Whatever was in that painting, I'm not that guy."

Danni opened her eyes again, confused. He didn't know?

"It *was* you, wasn't it?" he asked again.

Danni held a detached gaze on the building, then turned it out to the rest of Bluesland. The white sun blazed in the pale gray sky and hit the top of every building in the park. Danni could almost hear the tinny melody of carnival music, and beyond that the thrilled screams of children.

She stared back at the carousel. Who had painted that? And *why*?

"Let's go," she said finally. "I'm going to need your help with something first."

"Okay, I'll go put the fires out."

She stopped him with a hand on his shoulder. "Leave them. Maybe they'll burn the damn thing down."

Ten

The sign above the mirrored top rail read 'Three
hundred years, still the Same Day.' Below it, bottles of rum
stood in a faded row from light to dark. Christmas lights
hanging in the rafters lit the cobwebs in a smoky red glow.
The scent of sugar cane met the antiseptic tinge of green
soap somewhere around waist level while a tattoo gun
buzzed fresh ink into skin behind a red vinyl curtain.

"Welcome to Same Day. Buyin', sellin', drinkin' or
inkin'?"

The bartender's midriff top was little more than a shred
of gauzy black cloth held in place by four ties. Her eyes
darkened when she looked up and saw Danni.

"Don't do it," Danni warned.

"MAMA LOU!"

Danni frowned. "I told you not to do that."

The wet smack of the curtain pulled their attention to
the back of the room. Before Michael could make see the
shape coming toward them, Danni stepped in front of him.
She pressed a hard finger against his lips and issued a soft
but definitive command.

"Say. Nothing."

Mama Lou's voice sounded damp and full of gravel like someone had kicked her teeth down her throat. Her breasts came to rest against her lap, covered by a long dress printed in an outrageous gold pattern.

"Danielle."

"Lou." Danni settled a hand against her hip. "You're looking … well, at least you're still walking."

"*Malbonodora putino.*"

Danni shrugged. "Yeah, well, we can't all be pillars of virtue, can we?"

Mama Lou tossed a loose fistful of braids over her shoulder and then closed a tight fist in the air. Shutters snapped shut behind them, blotting out the sun and the sound of Bourbon Street. Mama Lou leaned out from the bar for a cleaner look at Michael.

"What'cha got there? A pet? Looks a little *white* for ya."

"Lou, meet Michael. Michael? Mama the Hutt. Don't say hi. She thinks she's cute because she can read auras, which when you think about it, Lou, is kind of the shallow end of the pool as far as gifted magic goes."

The bartender sailed over the oak bar with blades drawn in both hands. Danni felt the sweep at the back of her knees, the hard smack of her back against the floor, but she barely registered the blade at her throat as she spoke around a wheeze of laughter.

"Whitney, here, on the other hand, is *soldato*. A blood soldier."

Michael reached forward, but how far she couldn't see. Enough that Whitney pressed a matching knife against his groin.

Danni guided her eyes down to where the bone-handled

knife was positioned over Whitney's heart.

"*Ah-ah*, princess," Danni said. "That's Daddy's blade you're pushing into."

Whitney pressed her edge a little deeper. "So is this."

"And for which of us does that mean *lasting* damage?"

A few more moments passed in breathless silence. Whitney's eyes took another survey of the weapon resting in Danni's hand. Then slowly, inch by inch, she withdrew but not before hacking a wad of spit across the bridge of Danni's boot.

"*Putino.*"

Danni reached for Michael's hand and pulled herself upright again.

"You really need to mop that floor," she said.

The tattoo gun deeper in the shop stopped. The curtain slapped back again.

"What's with all the dark? Danni, girl!"

A man maneuvered around Mama Lou and Whitney, bringing with him the clatter of beads and bones sewn into his Naugahyde vest. A stack of copper bangles slipped down rawboned arms as he dove in for a tight hug.

"Carin," Danni grunted.

He pulled back, but his hands stayed on her upper arms, his voice low between them. "She ain't real moved 'bout you comin' here no more."

"She hasn't been moved since I came across the Twinspan."

Carin's nod was slow but conceding. "You be right 'bout 'at. Let's take dis 'round the back then."

He motioned them forward through the curtain. The room was transected by a gummy piece of duct tape. On one side, old iron basins held colanders of scarlet crawfish, while beside them big copper kettles simmered a different kind of heat into the air. Danni settled on the black bench against the opposite wall.

"Have a seat, cap," Carin said.

A low stool slid out toward Michael.

"Don't say much, do he?" Carin's mossy eyes shifted to Danni. "Then again, you ain't much for talkin' neither. And since your skins too pretty for inkin', and you ain't one for chattin', you're here on account of somethin' else." Carin slid up on the steel table with a wheezing groan. "So, what brings you in?"

"Paint, actually."

Something darkened in Carin's face. "Prolly ought to try Jackson Square."

Danni shook her head slow. "Different kind. Like the stuff someone might make from the drippings off all that meat."

Michael's eyes followed her finger to the long grease trays tucked beneath the griddles. Carin's did not. "Don't know what you might mean."

Danni offered him a dubious frown. "I know Mama Lou's kitchen when I smell it, Carin. It would have been enough to cover four walls, twice the size of this room."

Carin pushed himself off the table and busied himself with a wasted needles and spattered ink beside her.

"Man, wasn't nothin'. Couple of kids lookin' to scare up a little toby. Nothin' was gonna hurt nobody. They just kids. Ain't got nothin' better to do."

Spirit paintings. Go figure.

"What kind of toby?" Danni asked.

"Movin' kind. Can't none of them afford dat new Cineplex in the quarter. Said dey wanted to make dey own picture."

"How old?" she asked.

"Nine, ten. I dunno. Young enough trouble's all dey into most days. Every one of them already got ink on the back 'dey necks. Baby bangers at night, and by day pickin' scraps off Lou's dumpster when they can't get one dem nuns ta feed 'em."

"Nuns?" Michael asked.

"Dammit," Danni hissed and spun around to Michael.

Carin lifted his top lip and flashed a row of broken teeth.

"Well, well. He's still gotta tongue. Yeah, Cap, nuns. Carmelites runnin' in and outta here all times of day. Feedin' the po', clothin' the... naked, or whatever. Bad for bidness."

Danni held out a wide, cautioning palm toward Michael and asked, "What kind of bad?"

"Belle, please. You ain't been outta the game so long you don't know." Carin twisted back around to Michael. "But you look a little wet, so let me get it to you straight. Down here they be two kind a folk, da sinners and da saints. All them other little people in between? We just fightin' for dey money.

"Ever since the storm, we be gettin' made up by these outta-town good-doers. Movie stars and TV people come in and build 'eco-friendly' homes, tryin' to put airs on people ain't never had 'em. I'm damned tired of it. So, whatever insurance you in, we ain't buyin'."

"He's not selling insurance, Carin."

"He means *tariff*." The stool slid back as Michael drew upright, eye-to-eye with Carin. "The city keeps trying to chase you out, forcing you to pay them off. They've been trying to do it since Katrina. Trying to make N'awlins more palatable to outsiders. Hide the real crime so everyone feels safe. Close the real store and put up gift shops. And it

65

means you, Danni, Mama Lou, and the people like you, aren't welcome in your own city anymore."

The room seemed to breathe and settle as the tension unwound a half turn. Carin nodded once.

"Sounds 'bout the whole of it, Cap. 'Cept you got one thing wrong." He sucked air through a pitted incisor and tossed a chin toward Danni. "She ain't *never* been welcome here."

"Thanks," Danni murmured. She slid off the bench and gently eased them apart.

"The nuns, Carin. Would someone try to chase them off or… hurt them?" Danni asked.

"Can't say so. Houngans in the quarter ain't picky. A god's a god, no matter who be believin' in 'em. You know dat better than you should."

"A fair point," she said, "which brings me to my next favor."

"I ain't in the bidness of favors," he snapped.

"I need a bottle."

Carin shrugged. "Can't help you. Mama Lou be keepin' track of the spirits deese days."

Mama Lou's bark of laughter rattled something wet in her chest. Michael and Danni spun around to find her wedged in the doorway.

"Was waitin' for that. Oughta see the look on your face, *putino.*"

Danni didn't have to see it to feel the sour in the back of her throat or the painful twist in the corner of her mouth.

"What's your price?"

"You ain't got nothin' I want." A finger as knotted as Mississippi driftwood shot out from her meaty fist. "He might, though."

"*No.*"

Danni started forward, but Michael stepped between her and Mama Lou. He looked over his shoulder.

"Hang on," Michael said. "Let's at least find out what the lady has in mind. What *might* I be able to do for you, ma'am?"

"Well, look at you," Mama Lou drawled. "Large and in charge."

"Lou ..." Danni warned.

"Oh, now, don't you fret, *putino*. You need a little liquid courage. Me, I've got a want for something shiny. Like maybe that bit of dangly you're wearing."

"Dangly," Michael said. He reached for his neck. "You mean my cross?"

"What would you want with a crucifix, Lou?" Danni asked.

"I'm looking to expand my options." Mama Lou reached out of sight. Her hand came back with an amber wine bottle. She rested the fat end against the jamb. "You want this or not?"

Michael reached for the back of his neck, but Danni stopped him again.

"You don't have to give it to her," she whispered.

"Will it help?" he whispered back.

Mama Lou answered. "Ain't no other way to go where she needs to be."

"Then you can make it up to me," he told Danni.

The cross disappeared into the deep crease of Mama Lou's right hand. Her left shot the bottle at Danni with a little more force than necessary. Danni hooked her elbow in Michael's and led him quickly toward the door.

Before they left, Mama Lou's voice sang out a chuckling taunt.

"Pleasure doing bidness with you, boy."

Danni's neck burned for a full block back to the truck, and a niggling sensation of anticipation redoubled to dread.

"What was that about?" Michael asked.

"Another problem for another time," Danni said. "You still have access to that warehouse you took me to?"

"Sure. Why?"

She motioned to the truck but didn't offer further explanation before climbing inside.

Michael fiddled the little cluster of keys in his lap.

"Danni, back there. She called you–"

"I know what she called me," she growled. She let her voice soften before continuing. "It'll be better for you if you don't ask too many questions."

Michael opened his mouth, started to say something, and then thought better of it. Danni waved her hand toward the dashboard.

"Warehouse. *Drive.*"

Eleven

"Give me a minute and I'll get the lights."

Danni moved ahead of him into the cool darkness as she waited for the lights to snap on. There were traces of a party strewn around the room, glass beer bottles, empty pizza boxes and other trash. She swept the majority of it aside with the edge of her boot.

"Looks like someone else has been here," Michael said.

"Shut the door. Lock it." She gripped the center I-beam with both hands. It would have to do. She looked at him. "How are you at CPR?"

Michael dropped his keys on the card table and shrugged.

"I'm trained but it hasn't really come up before."

"Well, it's about to. Thirty compressions, two breaths. Got me?"

She walked off a wide circle and then stopped, calling him closer with a single finger. "I'll have about five minutes, which should be enough ..." She stared at the bottle in her fist. "... That is, if Mama Lou didn't give me a jug full of toilet water. And if the Baron's in a good mood.

69

Don't try to resuscitate me until then."

The bone-handled blade rolled across the back of her hand with precision skill, and she tapped the dull edge against the thickest part of the bottle. The clink sang out but died quickly in the tangle of overhead plumbing. She did it twice more and the amber spirits darkened to a thick, rich gold that seemed to glow on its own. She bit down on the cork and spat it off into the darkness, but his hand beat her mouth to the top of the bottle.

"Wait," he said. "The Baron? *The Baron Samedi?* What, you couldn't just go throw firecrackers at Satan?"

She smiled and felt the wickedness in the gesture. "Satan and I don't have the history that the Baron and I do." She upended the bottle, swallowing past the gag that followed. "Thirty and two. Got it?"

He took a deep breath. "Five minutes. Thirty and two."

With a hand on either side of his shoulders, she shook him once. "If you screw this up, I die." She waited for a second and then added, "and it will be your fault."

"Five minutes. Thirty and two," he repeated.

Danni took one last look at him, another long drag off the bottle. She touched the steel beam and smashed the bottle at her feet.

Glass, rum, and pennies exploded in all directions. Michael almost managed a full breath before Danni started to fall straight at him. He caught her under the arms, dragged her clear of the glass, and laid her down gently.

He checked his watch.

"Five minutes. Thirty and two. Five minutes. Thirty and two. Five minutes. Thirty and two."

It became his chant, a whispered recitation that barely tamped down his growing fear.

"Five minutes. Thirty and two. Five minutes. Thirty and

two."

He checked his watch again. She'd been down for three minutes. Maybe he should start the CPR?

No. She said five, she got five.

"Five minutes. Thirty and two. Five minutes. Thirty and two."

And then it was five minutes. Her head had turned, gravity already settling her into the ground. He straightened it, opened her mouth, and blew two quick breaths. Then he measured the compression point with his palm, overlapped his hands and leaned in. Down, release.

"*Ow!*"

Michael jerked his hand from her chest. Something had stabbed into his palm and left a dark red blood blister beneath the surface. He reached for her again and felt for the source. The hard point was seated in the center of her breastbone, like the head of a nail. He shook of the obvious question and focused on his task.

Down, release, down, release, counting off the thirty pumps. Two quick breaths and back into position. Down, release, down, release...

No sooner had Danni closed her eyes on Michael's worried face then she opened them to a bed of polished gravel. The clamor of voices moaned a desolate song. A thousand languages of a thousand different cultures culminating to say the same thing.

Help us.

It was a song the Baron seemed to regard with no more attention than elevator music.

"Well, *cher*. So soon?"

She lifted her head slowly and found him seated in his

throne. Long spires of bone gated the ground around him. He kicked back the rim of his hat with the tip of his cane and flashed a radiant grin, if evil could be radiant. "And to what do I owe it?"

She took her time to stand, knocking away a few pebbles that stayed with her. "Bluesland."

"Feeling nostalgic?"

"Michael showed me a carousel. The painting. You *promised* me ..."

The Baron leaned forward. "What, *cher*? What exactly did I promise you?"

"That you wouldn't say a word about what happened there."

"Aye. And I have not said ... one ... *word*." The Baron pinched his thumb against forefinger and pulled them across his lips. "But, the devil, as you say, is in such details."

Part of her wanted the weep. Another part, to fight. She split the difference and paced off a few short, frustrated steps in the grave path below his throne.

"I didn't kill those people! You did!"

The Baron shook his head, slow and sad. "Guilt does not become you, *cher*. But what does it matter? You've never been particularly concerned for those you've helped condemn."

Her thoughts flew to Michael. She'd tried to tamp down the curious mixture of rage and remorse that had moved to the forefront of her thoughts since they'd left the theme park. The anger might be warranted, but the other was far more complicated.

The Baron leaned over his knees. "Oh, oh. You care about what he thinks of you."

A hard, invisible jerk yanked her feet off the path and

dumped her directly in his lap. His arm snaked around her waist as he pinched the bottom of her chin. "The question is, *why?*"

Her reflection stared back from inside his amber eyes for what could have been a few seconds or an hour. She might already be dead. The thought of Michael's frantic breaths filling her lungs shook her away from the spell of the Baron's eyes long enough to disentangle herself from him. She shoved away his slow, encircling arm.

"We still have a deal, don't we?"

"Oh, yes." He tapped a finger against the head of the nail. The sensation rippled across her nerve endings, deep into her bones. "Have you figured it out yet? What it is that makes him different?"

He was toying with her, distracting her. The rum gave her the ability to travel to the Crossroads independent of the Baron, but she couldn't stay here indefinitely. She stumbled from his lap, but the Baron rose to pursue her. His white coat opened to a bare-skinned chest that rippled and spread. Faces formed under his skin, sliding back and forth across his ribs, down his stomach and lower.

He paced her down the limits of the Crossroads like some rehearsed dance that Danni knew would inevitably end with her in his arms again. She doubted she had the strength to tear herself away a second time.

Her hand slipped in her pocket and came back with two perfect pennies. They slid together between her thumb and forefinger. The Baron's eyes widened and he drew up short, captivated by the copper light that blazed between them.

"What do you think you're doing, *cher*?"

Danni knew he didn't want her answer so much as consider exactly what playing with the Father of the Death might cost.

She snapped both coins inside her fist. "Christopher Maurice Durrant."

The Baron made an angry noise but thankfully kept his distance as she lobbed them into the river of faces. The wall of the dead parted to blackness and a shade rose in the center, his young face pulling free of the others. He stared at her, then at the Baron, uncertain and more than a little confused.

"Am I …?"

"Dead. Your debt is paid," she told him. "You may leave this place. But first, I need to know how you died."

Christopher regarded her for a moment, the hollow pits where his eyes should have been searching for the memory. "I don't know," he said slowly.

"I put myself in a lot of danger to free you—"

"Oh, you have no idea," the Baron growled.

She ignored him and turned back to Christopher. "The least you could do is tell me what you remember."

Again, the spirit seemed to hesitate at the memory. He turned his translucent hands over in front of his face. "He was… big. Tallest man I've ever met. And he was singin'. *My gran'ma and your gran'ma were sittin' by the bayou…*"

The voices of the dead rose, one vaulted choir, anguished and off-key. Danni withered against them, feeling their pain as brilliantly as if it were her own. She heard women and men, but also children, voices lacking weight but still distinct among the concert.

"*Iko, Iko an deye. Jockamo fe nah ah na nay. Jockamo fe nah ah nay.*"

The song only contributed to the Baron's mounting fury. He beat them back, screaming words in a language she guessed hadn't been used in a few millennia. They

74

wailed and crashed back over each other.

Christopher rushed toward her, the bare hint of a body morphing into a trail of light and smoke that rushed high over her head. He stopped to look below him before racing toward freedom. Danni watched until he was a pinprick of light dissipating into a field of starless black. The voices faded away, and soon it was just Danni and one very furious Baron.

His bottomless voice came from everywhere and nowhere. "Happy now, *cher*?"

No answer was better than the wrong answer, and Danni stood stock-still, her perception of time lost. A very human part of her prayed that her five minutes was up.

"What have I told you about stealing from me?" he asked.

The Baron spun his cane on his fingertip and the dead erupted from the lake to form a wall behind her.

The white suit, the top-hat, and the cane melted away. The hard edges of The Baron's body began to ripple and reform in long lines of glittering smoke. He swelled into long tendrils that snaked around her waist, her legs, her wrists. Danni forced herself to relax.

To wait.

To breathe.

"Oh, no, *cher*." A sharp burst of smoke shoved past her lips, invading her mouth and throat. "You're quite done *breathing*."

She slammed her eyes shut. He shoved past her choking resistance. Danni held on the one hope she still had.

Thirty …

And two …

Thirty …

And two …

Twelve

Danni felt something slam against her chest. It sent her breath out in a painful rush. She struggled for air, found it hurt too much, and rolled loosely onto her side. A dull ache climbed up her spine and exploded over her head, thickening the sound of blood as it rushed between her ears. A warm hand rocked her face toward the light. She tried to sit upright but was immediately pushed back to the floor.

She coughed a long line of black slime. "I'm okay."

Michael wiped it away with his hand and then helped her up to rest on her elbows. "Oh yeah, never looked better. Hold it right there for just a second, don't try to sit up yet."

He rushed off into the darkness and then returned with a bottle of water. She reached for it and almost fell. He caught her with one arm and guided the bottle to her mouth.

"Take it slow."

She took a sip, then a longer drink.

"Good, let's see if we can get you sitting up now. I'm going to move you a bit."

Once she was resting against the post, he put the bottle in her hands. Everything hurt, her lungs, her legs, her head.

Another long round of coughing produced more black spit. Michael unfolded a handkerchief from his pocket and wrapped it around a couple of fingers. Gently, he wiped the stream of slime off her cheek.

"What is this stuff?" he asked as he flipped a hunk from her hair onto the floor.

"Bone dust," she wheezed. "We need to go."

"No, we need to talk. What the hell just happened? Why did I give Mama Lou my confirmation cross? And what the hell is wrong with your chest?"

A single eyebrow marched up her forehead. "Something wrong with my chest?"

"Well… not …I mean…" He extended two fingers in the space over her heart. "The part where it's nailed to your spine."

"Not nailed to. Nailed *through*." She caught his hand and moved it against the hard outline of the nail head. "Cold iron. About four inches."

Michael stared at the place where his fingertips met her skin, trying to make sense of what she was saying and what he felt.

"Does it hurt?"

She shrugged. "Going in."

"*Why do you have a nail in your chest?*"

"I suppose The Baron thought it was funny at the time."

"Sick sense of humor." Michael withdrew his hand and helped her back to her feet.

"Did you see him?" he asked.

"I did." She stepped off a few paces and kicked a hunk of amber glass against the wall. "Thank you, by the way."

"Sure. Does it earn me some answers now?"

She nodded once. "The kid from the wall. Durant. He was there. I think a bunch of them were, actually." She chewed her bottom lip thoughtfully. "It doesn't make sense."

"What about that doesn't make sense?" he pressed.

"The Baron can't collect children. He can't make deals with them either. But I could hear them, *see* them."

"Then how?"

"I'm not entirely sure."

Michael blew out a long breath and tucked his hands in his pockets. Something flashed in his eyes, a different kind of tension than she'd seen before, and when he spoke again, his voice was edged with frustration.

"Then let's go back. What's the deal with you and Mama Lou?"

Danni couldn't stop the smile from rising into her voice. "We have a history."

"You mean you used to work for her."

"We work for the Baron."

"Nobody works *for* the Baron. They serve." Michael started picking glass from the floor and flipping it into the trash, unable to keep the bitterness from his voice. "So, what's he got on you that put that nail in your chest?"

"I stole from him once. He hasn't seen fit to take it out since."

"And what does that even mean?"

"It *means* I can go places you can't. That's why you came looking for me in the first place, isn't it? Because I can do things you can't. And as far as I can see it, nothing I did before this moment is any of your damned business."

He slammed a fistful of glass into the trash. "It *is* my business. These are my people. My responsibility. And I'd at least like a heads up before you just …" He waved his hand at the damp stain on the cement. " … run off and visit the Crossroads!"

"You don't get to ask for my help and then dictate how I go about doing it!"

Danni blew out a long, calming breath and willed the anger out of her voice before moving into the full glare of the overhead lights.

"For whatever sick, twisted reason he has, he's allowing me to help you figure out what happened to your friends. So, my suggestion is that you let me before he changes his mind."

"I just brought you back to life! It doesn't matter to me what your past is, I'm not going to let you make some deal with the Baron to give it back to him."

Danni offered him a sad smile. "You don't really have a choice. I help you, he gets me. I don't? He still does. That deal is done."

Michael picked up a half empty beer bottle and weighed it in his hand. He tossed it in the air once and then threw it across the room. It shattered and splashed against the far wall. He watched as liquid ran in tiny rivulets to puddle on the floor. He looked at her again, but his expression was sad.

"You're welcome to stay at the convent as long as you need."

"Generous, but I won't be sleeping anytime soon."

She bent over her knees and drew a deep breath. She could still taste the Baron on her tongue, the sticky flavor of tobacco and burnt sugar. "He can find me in my dreams."

She grabbed his keys off the table and tossed them at his chest.

"Sun's setting. Let's go see what other kind of trouble I can get you into."

Thirteen

Michael guided the truck along the latticework of streets as the last bit of sun slipped from the sky. The pockmarked roads were dark except for the occasional stabs of a traffic signal. Somewhere up the road a fire hydrant had been opened and the run-off was deep around the drain. Water sluiced up the window as Michael made a rolling stop through a flashing intersection.

"Strangely quiet," Danni said as they passed row after row of darkened houses. "Ninety-plus degrees outside and those stoops aren't crowded with people?"

Instead, windows were pulled flush against the seals, shades drawn, and puckered down the seam. The fire escapes hung free from pitted brick walls. But that wasn't new. People didn't mind the possibility of dying in a fire if it meant avoiding the certainty they'd get robbed or worse.

"Been like this all summer," Michael said. "This was Sister Martine's neighborhood. She'd be out here, even in the worst heat."

"She's one of the …" Danni caught herself. "… missing?"

"Most recent one, anyway."

Danni scanned the narrow avenues between buildings. They were desolate apart from overflowing Dumpsters and the occasional burned-out sedan.

A flicker of movement caught her eye. A shadow broke the light between the slatted fencing farther down the egress. She lost sight of it around a burned-out brownstone but found it again in the next alley.

"Slow down."

The engine whined as Michael lifted his foot from the accelerator. The roar of passing air stilled and brought in the tinny melody of voices on the street.

"My pahrain told your pahrain, I'm gonna set your soul on fire."

"Listen! Do you hear that?" Danni asked.

Michael listened for a line. "They're singing."

Danni nodded. "Pull in the next alley."

He eased the truck across the culvert and beneath a low service overhang. The fence line broke from slats to chain link at the far end of the alley. Danni grabbed the edge of the window and pulled herself out and around the door. Her feet were running before the truck stopped. Her momentum sent her fast down the alley ahead of him. She caught the top of the fence and sailed over easily.

She closed the gap in less than a block. Proximity brought the shadows into clearer context. She counted at least eight children. When they veered down an alley she lost sight of them in a cloud of sewer steam. She raced through only to be met by a fist to the face.

Pain exploded across her jaw. She landed hard. Before she could recover, she felt herself hauled up only to be thrown back to the asphalt by another hard slam against her eye. The knife was in her hand, more reflex than reaction.

She swung it wildly and slashed at the broad shadow above her. When she connected, a warm splash of blood washed across her knuckles. A voice, dark and low, cursed at her in Creole before his receding footsteps echoed down the alley.

"Danni!"

Michael.

He looped his arms beneath hers and dragged her to her feet before settling her against the wall. She could barely make out the edges of his face.

"What happened?" he asked.

"They ran…that way. Follow them!"

"What? Why?"

"Just do it!"

He ran to the end of the alley and disappeared around a corner. A minute later he was walking toward her, out of breath.

"I don't see anyone. No kids, nobody," he said.

"They were right there!"

"You okay?"

She spit into her hand and ran it above her eye. "Yeah, come on."

He followed her back down the alley and into the street. She turned right and walked a few paces. He watched her stop on the curb.

"What are you—"

Danni raised a hand to stop him. She moved across the intersection then continued in a counter clockwise circle. She pointed down the street.

"There. I hear singing. Not as many this time. Seven … six."

She broke into a run again.

The farther they ran the worse the houses became. They passed a series of lots filled with broken bricks and debris.

He was just about to give in when Danni stopped. She raised her hand again and used the tip of the knife to indicate a house across the block.

He followed her between the piles of brick and stones. They skirted some fallen trees and a long discarded bathtub. He could hear the song again, but this time it didn't sound as friendly or as childlike as he had first thought. There was something flat and mechanical about the tones.

Danni raised the bone-handled knife and whetted it slowly along the wall. Sparks jumped from the blade but the sound was like the shriek of a vulture from the far end of a dark canyon.

The song died. Danni cocked her head and listened to the air. She smelled something dank and wet, muddy like the spring riverbank.

She started around the corner when a boy headed in the opposite direction collided with her. She staggered back a step, more startled than moved. He stared up at her wide-eyed, terrified then relieved. His eyes rolled back in his head and he collapsed at her feet.

She gave Michael a gentle backwards glance and then moved into long grassy pasture. It was vacant except the rustle of tall grass springing upright in the wake of something much larger. Her stooped to the grass and pressed her fingers into the wet mud. Blood.

When she looked back, Michael was holding the boy against his chest but scanning the empty lot.

"Where'd they go?" he asked.

She wiped her hand against her jeans and shook her head.

"How is he?"

"I'm not sure. His pulse is racing, but I think he's

asleep."

She lifted the boy's foot and inspected the bottom of his sneaker.

"Kid likes to run. No tread left on his toes."

She touched his neck and felt for his pulse. Michael was partially correct. She searched for the tingle, the rush of heat up her elbow, but found nothing. His soul was gone, but he was still breathing.

Her fingers pushed his head to the side. "Looky there. Tattoo. Any idea who he is?"

Michael sighed and shook his head. "No, but I know someone who might."

Fourteen

Michael insisted it was easier to walk rather than double-back around to the truck. He led Danni through yards and down to a small park. A merry-go-round sat still in tall grass. There was no game to interrupt in the small basketball court and clearly hadn't been in a while. Sprouts of burdock and wild onions trimmed the black top edges and a deflated ball looked partially melted into the asphalt.

Danni pushed back a section of the gap-linked fence to allow Michael, still holding the boy, ahead of her. He moved toward the wild hedge at the end of the park but stopped suddenly, causing Danni to run into him.

A tall black man eased down the steps of a modest frame house. His white cotton slacks matched his wide-brimmed Panama hat, white on white split by a black, Dixieland jacket. He tipped the hat to an elderly woman at the top of the steps.

Michael waited until the man rounded the far corner before taking a full breath.

"Someone you know?" Danni asked.

Michael kept his voice low. "You could say that. How

about you? You know him?"

"No, but he reminds me of someone I hate." She searched the edge of Michael's face in the near darkness. "I take it he just left where we're going?"

When Michael rang the bell, it echoed all the way to the back of the cottage. The patter of small footsteps followed the sound to the front window where half a weathered face and a bright blue eye peered through a sliver in the curtains before the old wooden door creaked open.

"Well now, Michael Belew, look at you."

The voice came from somewhere under a mountain, sounding more like a chain smoking ogre than the four-foot wisp of a woman behind the screen door.

"Sister Ned, you're looking well."

"You never were a good liar," she answered. "Who've you got there?"

Michael turned so she could see the boy's face. "We were hoping you could tell us."

"Gabriel." The nun pushed back his hair when he didn't stir. "Where'd you find him?"

"He kind of ran into us. Been asleep the whole way here." Michael adjusted the boy in his arms. "And he's starting to get heavy."

"You'd best come in then."

Sister Ned led them through a modest living room and down a short, wide hallway. She didn't bother with the light as she motioned Michael toward the narrow bed. Once Gabriel was settled, Michael rejoined the women in the hallway.

"He lives in a group home down the block," Sister Ned said. "I'll call them."

"Maybe after we talk for a bit?" Michael suggested. Sister Ned nodded slowly, clearly suspicious. Michael added, "Can't hurt to let him dream a bit."

"I'm not sure he's dreaming," Danni said.

Michael glanced back into the bedroom where Gabriel's eyes bounced side to side behind his eyelids.

"Michael, where are your manners?" Sister Ned asked.

"Oh, sorry. Sister Ned, this is Danni. She … she's here to help."

Sister Ned gave Danni an appraising look before nodding. "Well then, it seems we have things to discuss. I've some tea, if you'd like." As they stepped into the front room, Sister Ned's voice returned to full volume. "Or maybe something a little more … serious?"

"Whatever you're having," Michael said.

"More serious it is, then. Go on, get comfortable. I'll be along."

Michael took the far end of the couch while Danni circled the room, stopping at the window overlooking the street and pushing back the edge of the curtain with her finger.

"Something out there?" Michael asked softly.

Her voice stayed tight in the back of her throat. "I'm certain of it."

Sister Ned returned with three bottles of Amber-Bock and a church key. Popping the caps, she handed a bottle to each of them and then settled into a rocking chair with her own.

"Hope you don't mind. Don't much care for dirtying dishes just to look fancy." She took a long pull from the bottle and held it up. "Besides, this is a better use for water. So, my dear, what's your story?"

Michael leaned forward. "Sister Ned, we just wanted to ask you—"

Her hand came up to stop him. "You'll get your turn.

Sit quiet and let the ladies talk."

Michael watched as Danni moved back around the room, to the opposite end of the couch. Sister Ned offered her a soft smile.

"I am Sister Natalia Robicheaux, but that's a mouthful, ain't it? Sister Ned'll do. May I call you Danni?"

"At least until you get to know me."

"*Ah,*" Sister Ned said, "So you're her. Should have seen it right off. Strong shoulders, strong legs. Walk around with a confident grace, but you got all that pain in your eyes."

Danni bristled, but the old sister held her gaze.

"Reverend Mother's words," Sister Ned explained.

Danni sniffed. "She's not my biggest fan."

Michael sat forward. "I didn't realize the two of you had met."

"Just long enough for her to remind me to be on my *best* behavior."

He started to say something, but Sister Ned cut him off again. "You know Reverend Mother isn't too keen on all this, Michael. That's alright, though. It's not the kind of plan she *should* be keen on. But she trusts you. *I* trust you."

"And me?" Danni asked.

Sister Ned hesitated, as if considering her words carefully. "Michael trusts you. I assume you're here to help. That's enough for me."

Danni relaxed into the couch. "Then tell me what's happening in your parish, Sister."

"We used to have these card games here at the house," Sister Ned began. "Poker. Seven card stud, hold 'em, high Chicago." Sister Ned scoffed at Michael. "Don't sit there with that surprised look on your face, Mister 'I swapped the sacramental wine with grape Kool-aid to impress a girl.' Besides, we're not gambling. Whatever we win goes into the collection box. We're just doing math to decide who gets to give the usher the biggest tip each week."

Sister Ned's face darkened. "Two of them, Sister Marie Alvarez and Sister Salvatore, disappeared a few weeks ago. They aren't at home. They aren't at the convent, or at church. They're just … *gone*."

Danni's gut twisted on itself. "Any idea who would want to hurt them?"

"You're assuming they're hurt," Michael interjected, but there was a question just below the surface of his words. One Danni felt compelled to answer, but was still uncertain if she should.

"Danni," he pressed.

Thankfully, Sister Ned stopped him. "Michael."

Spoken as such, his name contained a cautious warning but also an acute awareness. Danni felt Sister Ned's cool, intuitive eyes tracking every expression, and she wondered if the old nun already understood what she wasn't saying. Sister Ned took a long pull off her beer before continuing.

"Can't say as I know anyone who'd want to bother those two, or any of the others, for that matter. Sisters St. Jude and Cecilia are younger, so they work a little more directly with the people. Local co-op, food pantry, but mostly child-care. Sister Martine is our senior outreach missionary. She has a tendency to rub up some fur, but mostly city officials. No one who'd actually harm her."

"You think something else is going on," Danni said, more as an observation than a question. Sister Ned answered it anyway.

"My back door is off the kitchen, and it's two steps to the alley from there. Used to be, the local kids, like Gabriel, would come by for lunch. I'd give them a bit extra to take home to their brothers or sisters … or mothers. Now, maybe two or three a day come by. Some of them only once a week. All of them have this fear in their eyes. They're polite, but short, looking over their shoulders even while they're saying thank you. I figured it was gang stuff. Maybe some 'bangers waiting in the street to take the food off them.

"I asked one of them, a young kid, Pero Castillo. He used to come every day. He's feeding two sisters and a baby brother with what I'm giving him. Usually I make him eat here before I let him leave with anything. Lately he says no, he can't stick around. Lord, I can see how hungry that boy is. But he won't wait. Says he has to be back before nightfall."

"Did he say why?" Danni asked.

Sister Ned finished her beer. "Said there was this shadow man in the street, waiting for kids to step out of line."

"And normally your sisters would be out there, watching over them," Danni finished.

Sister Ned's nod was swift. "Parents are a rare commodity around here. Most of these kids come from broken homes, one parent if that. We do our best to protect them, but this shadow man wants to find them alone. According to Pero, he's using a song to bait them."

Michael looked at Danni. "They were singing Iko, but we didn't see anyone."

No, because she got punched in the eye. But someone else had been in that alley. She was sure of it.

"Best guess," Danni explained, "he's using Iko as his *gachèt*, his trigger. To you or me it just sounds like music, but it puts them in a trance. Lets him control them somehow. Gabriel and the others weren't running away from something, they were running *toward* it. We just happened to interrupt."

Michael looked at Sister Ned again. "If that's the case, how is Pero still around to tell you about it?"

Sister Ned shrugged. "He said that he was out late, running an errand for his mother when he heard it. He said he doesn't know how long, he lost all track of time. But a garbage truck came around a corner and almost hit him. The horn startled him awake. When the horn stopped, the music was gone. He took off running for home."

Sister Ned stopped, clearly struggling to make sense of it herself. She picked at the peeling label on her beer. In the silence, Danni could hear the clock ticking in the kitchen, and Gabriel singing softly in his sleep.

She tossed a thumb over her shoulder to the bedroom. "What do you know about the tattoo on his neck?"

"A number of the children have them," she answered. "I figured it was part of some kind of gang initiation, but none of them would say."

"Christopher Durant? Did he have one?" Danni asked Michael.

He shrugged, but Sister Ned nodded slowly.

"Yes, I think he did," she answered. "Where'd you run into Christopher?"

Danni shook her head and pressed on. "Did he live at the same group home as Gabriel?"

Again, the sister nodded. "Christopher and Gabriel were part of a group of children whose families didn't make it to the shelters before the storm hit. Honestly, can't say where most of them came from. Lot more orphans came out of that summer than the city would have you believe."

Danni sank forward with her head in her hands. "I was afraid of that."

Eventually, she stood and moved back to the bedroom door. She drew the knife from her waistband and thumped it against her hip. Gabriel's finger twitched once, then again, each time as she thumbed the blade. She closed her eyes and worked her mind back to the Crossroads and the song she'd heard there. Her voice whispered into the room.

"My pahrain and your pahrain, sittin' on the bayou…"

On the bed, Gabriel's thin voice finished the verse. "My pahrain told your pahrain, I'm gonna set your soul on fire."

Danni pushed herself away from the wall but didn't sit again. Instead, she sucked back the beer until her stomach was heavy and warm. Finally she cast a long, sad look in Michael's direction.

"I heard Gabriel's voice in the Crossroads. I heard a lot of them there."

"You said children don't go to the Crossroads."

"I said *usually*."

Danni wet her lips to continue, but the words died before they made it out of her throat. She shook her head and paced the length of the small living room. Michael exchanged wary glances with Sister Ned, who reached for the rosary on her hip and motioned Danni toward the couch. "If you've got a confession to make, child, you're in good company."

"I don't know that it will make much sense to either of you," Danni said.

Sister Ned only shook her head. Still, Danni hesitated, considering the old nun and then Michael. Where did she begin? She let out a long sigh and moved back to the couch.

"Shortly after Katrina, The Baron told me about some houngans who had made deals with him and then defaulted in some way or another. They were all hiding out in the same place, using his own magic against him to keep him out. And doing a damn good job of it."

The air left Michael's lungs around a single word. "Bluesland."

Dimly, she continued. "I didn't know at the time it wasn't just the people who owed him, but their whole families. He sent me in to collect. Once I opened the barrier they'd put up to stop him and Samedi got in, he …" She swallowed the tension in her throat. "He slaughtered them. He didn't have to, but he was enraged. It happened so fast, and there were so many of them, running and screaming. As he killed them, he pulled out their souls and trapped them…"

She let the thought die, watching the memories surface behind her eyes as clear and brilliant as the toby painted inside the carousel. Violent flashes and screams, undercut by the Baron's wicked laughter. The smell of blood and the sound of crying children. It flooded back, not in waves, but a deluge of sights and sounds, each one more awful than the next.

When she looked at him again, Michael's green eyes were steeped in horror.

"I wanted to tell you, but…" He'd been so convinced she was a hero, had *been* a hero, when in actuality, she was an agent of destruction.

Her guilt redoubled when Michael waved off her words, clenching his jaw and taking an audibly deep breath before speaking again. "Just tell me the rest."

"When the Baron was done with the adults, he turned on the children. I begged him to let them go. They were so scared, I … they'd already watched their parents being murdered, and I … "

Michael sat silent as she struggled for words. Danni felt

Sister Ned's warm, assuring hand touch her knee. "Go slow. What happened next?"

She could no long look at Michael and resigned herself to focus on Sister Ned. "For whatever reason, the Baron can't make deals with children. But when he claimed Bluesland, he said they were already part of it. Whatever magic their parents had used to keep him out bound the children there. He let them live, but he took their souls."

"You watched," Michael growled.

"What choice did I have?" she begged.

"Not letting him into a Bluesland, for a start!"

The warm hand left Danni's knee, and a finger shot out from Sister Ned's fist. "Do not judge," she said sharply, "and you will not be judged. Do not condemn, and you will not be condemned."

Michael's gaze dove toward the floor, staring at his hands for a long minute. He flexed them to fists then released them, over and over, until he looked at Danni again with genuine regret in his eyes.

"Forgive, and you will be forgiven," he finished, though he seemed to be having a difficult time with the concept. "I'm sorry."

For what, Danni wasn't entirely sure. She deserved a little judgment. Maybe a lot. Still, Sister Ned's words seemed to settle his anger for the moment.

Danni released a long, slow breath. "To be honest, I didn't really know what happened to them until today. Though, who would want them dead now—"

"That should seem obvious," Michael said.

Danni shook her head. "They're more valuable to him alive." Absently, she touched the nail head in the center of her chest. "We all are. Whoever this ... shadow man is, he's inviting Samedi's wrath, which might be why he encouraged me to help you in the first place."

Michael said nothing, but the idea unsettled him. In using Danni's help was he, by extension, helping the Baron to secure his power? He started to address it aloud when a thin voice pulled their attention to the bedroom doorway.

"S-sister Ned?"

Michael and Danni stood simultaneously. Danni immediately noticed the golden hue in Gabriel's eyes, almost the color of pale honey against his dark skin. His gaze stayed locked on Danni, more awestruck than afraid. How much of their conversation he'd heard, she could only guess.

"Gabriel?" Sister Ned asked, but he didn't seem to want her anymore.

"We followed the shadow man," he said. "He was singing, and he said we could sing, too. We were singing with him in the field, until the demon came."

"Demon?" Danni asked. "What kind of demon?"

Gabriel's eyes dove to his feet where he toed the rug. "It took Domo and Tia. It took everybody. It was going to take me, too, but then I ran. And I found you. And you saved me … again."

Danni's eyes went wide. She stared at Michael and saw understanding come into his eyes.

"Gabriel, you were at Bluesland, right? With your parents?" he asked.

He nodded. "My mom. But the monster took her. It took everybody. But then she came." His finger shot out to Danni. "She chased it away, like she chased away the demon."

Before she could react, Gabriel rushed toward her. His arms locked around her waist, and he pressed his face into her stomach. She held her arms away from her body and shot a pleading look at Michael, who only smiled and rested a shoulder against the wall.

When Gabriel withdrew, Danni eased him back a few steps and knelt in front of him. "Gabriel, I didn't—"

Doe eyes stared back at her, glistening with devotion and unshed tears. She glanced at Sister Ned for help

"Come here, boy," Sister Ned said.

He trudged across the room to Sister Ned, who set her hands against his shoulders.

"How about you stay with me for awhile? Miss Danni's got some work to do."

Gabriel looked over his shoulder at Danni. Not knowing what else to do, she nodded at Gabriel.

Sister Ned raised a finger in front of him. "But, same rules as at the school. Right?"

"Yes, ma'am."

"Starting now. Go wash those hands. Bathroom's that way."

Gabriel gave Danni one last look before trotting off down the hall.

"All right. I'll take him," Sister Ned said, as if there was a question to the matter. "Maybe he's right. Maybe I can't take care of all of them. But I can take care of Gabriel."

Michael bristled. "Who said you couldn't?"

"Brother LaCroix. He was here just before you."

"*Brother* LaCroix?" Michael repeated.

"Yes, you must've passed him on the street. He provides services for a number of funeral homes in the city. Opened a new one in fact, right next door to Holy Cross cemetery. He left me several business cards." She picked one up from the coffee table and handed it to Michael.

"Strange name, though. 'Eternal Commitments.' But, if

he's doing the Lord's work … "

Fifteen

Danni ticked the edge of her knife against her thumb while Michael kept his eyes on the road. His knuckles tightened then released, flaking the sun-faded foam under his palm. They shared the silence, using the time to reflect on their own demons before hunting up new ones.

"So, seems like you're not the only one who recalls certain events differently," Michael said softly. "How's it feel to be someone's hero?"

Did he mean Gabriel's or his? The answer was the same either way.

"Undeserved." She readjusted in the seat to see him more clearly. "I don't even know where to begin with Gabriel, but you should know, no matter how many Bible verses Sister Ned quotes at you, you're not wrong to be angry with me for what I did."

"Maybe," he agreed, "but anger almost always comes from fear. Let me ask you this. Knowing what you know now, would you do it differently?"

She shrugged. "I'd have to go back a bit further than Bluesland to undo a lot of it, but, yes, I would."

"There you go then. Just don't help the Baron steal any more souls."

Danni winced. "It's *really* not that simple. We're not friends or business partners. The Baron *owns* me. Truly and irrevocably. What I do for him now means I might not spend eternity as his bitch."

Michael didn't offer any further debate as he worked the truck down through the gears and cruised up to another flashing intersection. The glove compartment popped open as the truck jumped off the line. Piles of papers spilled across Danni's feet. The more she tried to cram it back into the dash, the faster it fell. Finally she gave up and shoved her hand deep inside, only to find a plastic clown toy, a crowd pleaser tossed from a Mardi Gras float. She squeezed it once and it let out a sharp, piercing squeal. It's painted red eyes and blue mouth shot out from its head, only to be sucked back as her hand relaxed. Danni felt the smile building in the corner of her mouth.

"You really swap out the sacramental wine to impress a girl?" she asked.

He nodded. "Paid penance for it, too. Couldn't sit for two days."

"Must've been a pretty girl."

Michael flashed a quick smile at her. "The ones who get me in trouble usually are."

The truck slowed and Michael eased it to the curb at the corner of the street. He jerked the parking brake and leaned over the steering wheel.

Eternal Commitments sat at the end of the block. Ground lights cast long shadows up a row of pillars outside the iron doors that were as ornamental as they were secure. The building itself was a blister of white limestone amid a veritable wasteland of vacant lots and houses rocked sideways on their foundations.

The cemetery yawned in the distance. Long lines of mausoleums broken by the pointed tip of a few obelisks. Where those ended a field of white crosses stood watch over the dead who never made it into the ground or couldn't have afforded a headstone if they had.

Danni's eyes shifted back to Michael. "You know this Brother LaCroix?"

"You could say that."

"You seemed pretty pissed he stopped by Sister Ned's. He gonna be a problem?"

"Probably, but not the way you're thinking. What I can't figure out is why he'd set up shop *here*. This place has been shut down for years. The archdiocese buried sisters here mostly, some priests, the occasional bishop. But they don't use it anymore, not even for walking tours."

"Wanna go take a look then?"

"Sure, but maybe you should take this."

He pressed something in her hand. Her fingers curled instinctively around the cold trigger of a pistol.

Danni frowned at the gun in her fist. "I thought you said LaCroix wasn't *this* kind of trouble."

"He's not, but he's got people who are."

Danni checked and rechecked the safety before wedging it into the tight space between her hip and jeans.

She followed him to the end of the sidewalk, just beyond the glowing field of landscaping lights. They waited in the shadow, watching, listening, but she was more interested in what she didn't hear. No birds squabbling over trash. No crickets sizzling and clicking in the straw grass. This time of year the night should have been alive with a thousand remixes of the same song: "Its Fucking Hot." But the street was unduly quiet except for the gentle scratch of their footsteps.

Danni pressed her hand into the crumbling side of a vacant shop. Loose tar tile crumbled under her hand. A six-inch gouge traveled through to the underlying frame. Her hand ran over the depression and then farther down the building where she found four more. Her eyes searched the long corridor of shadows but found no distinguishable shape. She reached back for Michael but kept her attention trained on the alley. She lifted her fingers to her nose.

"There's blood on this wall," she whispered.

"There's more on the curb," he said.

A purplish stain encircled a full section of sidewalk.

"Nothing loses that much blood and survives," she whispered. "And whatever made these marks was wider than a hand. Maybe a rake or a garden tool."

"Or claws," he suggested.

She swallowed hard. "I'm liking this less and less."

"Me, too. Let's keep moving."

Michael stayed on point as Danni held back, blading her body to keep her eyes on the open ends of the street.

It wasn't the cemetery that unnerved her but the coverless expanse of the funeral home. The white-rocked flower beds full of hostas and climbing wisteria provided no safety against whatever had spilt all that blood.

A quick few steps took them past the funeral home and to the edge of the cemetery. The footpath split in two different directions. Night blended the trees into a long line of wispy shadows at the farthest end, while tombs lined the roadway down the other. Narrow staircases led to mourning benches. Copper doors, now green with age, held locks that hadn't been turned in a hundred years. The waterline was still faint around the upper half of the monuments. Danni tried to read the named as they passed, but most of them were washed out.

A thud whirled them both around.

"What was that?" Michael asked.

"Don't know. But it sounded heavy."

The farther they went, the taller the perimeter fence got. The posts alternated between wrought iron pickets and spear-tips. Michael stayed on the path for a hundred feet and then broke across the grass. She nearly tripped over the flat marble cenotaph of the Marlow family.

"You've been here before," she said as he deftly sidestepped the low remains of another footstone.

"Many times. Mostly during the day."

"Where are we going, then?"

"The center is a quarter mile northeast. If LaCroix is up to something, that's where it will be."

He led them along another winding path that climbed a steep embankment. She kept pace with him easily until they stopped just beyond the mausoleum on top of the hill. It was stylish, seated on a bed of white gravel and surrounded by black, marble coping, the crypt itself was made of heavy Portland stone. Most of the sheen had been worn away to expose the fossils trapped inside the rock. Danni whistled, long and low, but Michael's eyes narrowed with caution.

"What's wrong?" she asked.

"It's new."

"The mausoleum?" She glanced at the faded patina encrusted on the narrow doors, and then shook her head. "I doubt it."

"I'm telling you, *it's new*. Maybe not to this world, but definitely to this spot."

Danni stepped up to the door. She rattled the handle but it didn't budge. The stained glass doors were intact, but the leaded trim had been pulled away from the threshold. A swift kick sent a rattling echo across the grounds. She planted her boot against it two more times until finally it fell back into the narrow vault. She turned to Michael, victorious, but she only found panic in his face. He waved her forward.

"Make it quick. If someone didn't know we were here before, they sure do now."

The smell of mold and decaying bone was thick. All the vaults looked intact. Nameplates fit over the narrow cutouts in the wall, housing what she guessed to be bodies. Danni ducked the low lintel and drew upright in the faint glow that filled the tiny space. Her eyes roamed over the walls, the ceiling, searching for a light source but found none. In fact, it seemed like it was coming from everything.

A pedestal sat against the farthest wall, holding either a book or a box. Its top was smooth and soft like leather stretched taut over a square base. The sides were stapled with round white rivets. The pattern in the top was the same squiggly lines she'd seen marked across a hundred graves in the quarter. She held it close to her ear and shook it twice.

Nothing.

"What did you find?" Michael demanded.

"I dunno. It's a … thing. Looks pretty harmless. So it'll probably kill us." She passed it into his waiting hands. "Look like anything you've ever seen?"

Michael turned it over and made the same careful observation she had.

"Definitely not Catholic. There's a slit in the top." Michael worked his finger over the leather. "Let me use your knife?"

At least he'd asked this time. Michael cradled the box against his body, using his thumb to make one final pass over the opening before guiding the tip of the blade into it. Danni watched as it disappeared all the way to the hilt. Michael waited, gently twisting the handle this way and that before deciding whatever it needed, he didn't have.

"I guess you're—"

A strange heat flooded over her face. A pursuing boom made her ears pop. Danni was weightless for a moment, floating away from the ground as it changed directions beneath her. But she wasn't airborne long enough to know how. Her head stuck first, followed by her body. It was like being hit on all sides. She rolled across the surrounding headstones. Something made a terrible sound when it slammed into a limestone wall, and she realized it was her.

Danni lifted her head from the grass. Michael was twenty feet from her. His face was caught in the half light of passing shadows, but his expression was slack, his green eyes fatally empty. His hands clutched the box as screaming light rushed up and out. She'd heard those sounds before, though never quite so doleful and certainly not in this world.

"*Michael!*"

The squall of the voices increased. Fresh pain rocketed around inside her body. She stayed prone and made her way toward him on hands and knees.

As quickly as it had begun, it stopped.

Michael collapsed to his knees, the box tumbling away. Danni scrambled for him, catching his shoulders as he sagged toward the damp grass. She lifted his face to see a drunken stare blotted across his eyes.

"You ripped your shirt," he said.

"I didn't rip my shirt, the obelisk I hit on my way down did. What the hell was that?"

"I don't… I'm not sure."

She pulled them both to their feet. "Come on. We have to get you out of here. To a doctor, or a hospital, or a priest or something."

She looped his arm over her shoulder, half-walking, half-dragging him down the embankment. Michael began to laugh, his head lolling against her shoulder.

"Danni, I *am*—"

A hunk of limestone struck the ground beside her. A statue, or at least, part of one, stared up at them. Another blind volley whistled through the air. Danni only had a second to guess which direction it was coming from. She dove right and took them both back to the ground as the headless body of Jesus Christ tumbled by.

"Safe to say we're no longer alone," she said.

And whatever had joined them wanted them out... *now*. She hauled Michael to his feet again.

"Which way?" she demanded, suddenly lost in the maze of headstone and mausoleums.

The pointed top of an obelisk pierced the ground. Her hand wrenched around the collar of Michael's shirt. She broke into a run, no longer caring which direction they went as long as they were moving.

She drew the gun from her waist and fired blindly behind them. The first bullet landed in the mud with a sharp *whap!* But the second connected with something. Whatever it was, it shrieked, sharp and shrill. The noise rebounded against the maze of marble walls.

More stones flew from behind them, striking close enough to send marble dust into her face. She vaulted the lower headstones and darted between the ones she couldn't. She didn't chance a look behind them. She had to keep her eyes ahead of them as headstones appeared in the darkness, leaving her barely enough time to avoid them. Michael tripped along at an awkward pace, slowing them both.

"Left. Go left," he said.

It took them off the grass and back to the path. A pair of stone angel wings flew over her left shoulder and planted themselves into the ground. She made a minor correction to avoid them and ran hard against the pain in her legs.

As they approached the fence again, she felt her strength waning. Her boots were heavy and clotted with mud. Michael waited for her to make the first leap, which was less of a leap and more of a careful extraction. He followed, breaking into a run beside her as they started to clear the open grounds of the funeral parlor. She could see the outline of the truck in the distance with what little light there was reflecting off the windshield. They'd be safe if they made the truck.

Danni had little time to recognize the Panama hat gleaming bone-white as Brother LaCroix stepped from the iron doors of the funeral home. She threw on the brakes, sliding to a halt in the loose gravel of the flowerbeds, with Michael and the armless body of an angel only seconds behind her.

Sixteen

LaCroix stepped past them, and his hand shot out to swat the statue to the ground.

"Enough!"

The stone crumbled and scattered, clouding up dust that covered them all before settling again. LaCroix brushed alabaster dust from his collar and narrowed a set of pale blue eyes on Michael.

"I see you got my card, boy."

Michael panted for a clean breath, bent over with his hands on his knees. "Yes, Sister Ned … delivered … your message."

He straightened up as he felt the weight returning to his voice. "Are you using the innocent and aged now?"

LaCroix spread his hands in a wide, showy gesture. "I use what presents itself." He looked pointedly at Danni. "Can't say that I approve of your choice of tools, though."

"I'm nobody's tool," Danni said.

The smile on LaCroix's face could have meant anything, or just one thing. "Come now, my dear. We are all someone's device."

She pressed her hands to her back and held a long stretch, shifting her bones back into alignment.

"And you?" She closed the distance between them, moving into his face. "What kind of *tool* are you?"

"Danni, wait—" Michael started.

LaCroix cut him off. "Down boy. You put his *piece* in play. Let's see how well it serves you." He centered his focus on Danni. "I am a creature of my own making, *cher*. You really want to test me?"

"You're a—" Danni swallowed the words and staggered backwards.

LaCroix's smile got even wider, as if the bones and teeth had reordered themselves behind his lips. His face became a carnival expression of death, and his eyes began to glow like he'd called forth the embers of some unending cold fire.

"She's smart, this little *piece* is, Michael." His hands began to move in slow, tight circles around each other, fingers molding air, shaping a whirlwind between them. "But you could do better."

The earth beneath them rumbled. Michael searched for the source and realized the monuments were rising up and gathering around them. They pulled themselves from the earth and hung, suspended in the air above, with no question as to who was controlling their trajectory.

A voice came from somewhere behind Michael. "A moment, brother."

It sounded older than the rocks beneath their feet, but also thin and brittle like the flowers dried on a grave. Michael turned to look but saw only shadow and the moonlight reflected off the trees.

A small man appeared between them in faded farmer's overalls and a worn chambray work shirt. He leaned against a long-handled shovel with a small smile on his wrinkled, ebony face.

"I believe you're overstepping your ground, shall we say?"

It was phrased as a question that already had an answer. The fire was still in LaCroix eyes, but his face said the fight was over.

"I believe you are correct at this moment, Brother Cemetrie."

LaCroix swirled his hand in the air. The stone monuments above them evaporated only to reappear in their original places.

LaCroix looked at Michael. "Mind your tools, boy. Well begun don't mean done."

He reached out and gently swept a lock of Danni's sweat-damp hair from her eyes. "Another time, girl."

He lifted his hat and swept it down to his chest. In the time it took for it to pass over his face, LaCroix's body had vanished. Only his eyes remained, burning for several seconds after the rest of him was gone.

Cemetrie cackled. "Brother LaCroix do like to make an exit, don't he?"

Danni did a double take, looking to Michael then Cemetrie and back again.

"Before I pop off and get myself in more trouble," she said. "Who are you exactly?"

"Ah. I am the Baron Cemetrie." He swept Danni's hand to his lips. "I hold dominion over all of the cemeteries in the Delta. These poor folks around you, their bodies, their stones. In return, they do my bidding. Not Brother LaCroix's." He nodded ever so slightly at Danni. "And not Brother Samedi's. Now, if you'll excuse me. I have some clean up to do."

"Whoa. Wait a minute!" Danni said. "What the hell was chasing us?"

Cemetrie stared back into the dark edge of the cemetery, as if he could see something they could not.

"Eh, don't you worry 'bout him none." He flicked his hand, dusting them off like unwanted guests. "Go on, now. *Get.*"

Seventeen

"You're back."

Mother's Superior's voice was full of … something, but Michael had never been particularly good at differentiating between her annoyance and her surprise.

It might have been too much to hope that she wouldn't come find him the moment he returned to the convent. Too many years in shared dormitories had sharpened her awareness to fine needles, perceptive even in the deepest sleep.

Her footsteps were whispers against the kitchen floor as she moved to the opposite side of the stainless steel table, watching him.

"It looks like you've had an interesting evening," she said.

He continued to arrange food across the tray. "You could say that."

"You took her to see Sister Ned."

His eyes pulled up from the tabletop.

"You threatened her."

She scoffed. "You could hardly call that a threat."

"She's here to help us."

"All of us?"

Michael dropped the loaf of bread in his hand and pushed back the hair from his face.

"I'm honestly too tired for you to be so cryptic. If you have something to say, say it."

The barely pleasant tenor dropped from her voice. "You look a mess."

"I just got chased out of a cemetery by Lord knows what and directly into—" He let out a long breath. "Never mind. Suffice it to say, I'm tired, hungry, and I have a half dozen more problems than I started the day with. So, yes. I'm a mess."

"Perhaps if you spent more time in reflection than in action," she suggested.

He jerked the tray from the table a little harder than necessary. An unpeeled orange jumped off the edge and rolled across the floor.

"I've had enough reflection, thank you."

Her voice stopped him again at the door.

"There are still rules in this convent, Michael. I shouldn't have to remind you of that."

His chin turned against his shoulder, but didn't move to face her. "What rules are you referring to?"

She stepped into his periphery and set the orange on the tray again.

"Perhaps her bedroom is not the best place to dine."

Michael stared into the common room. The dining hall wasn't uncomfortable. He'd salvaged most of the chairs from the storm, and those he couldn't, he'd remade. Tables, too. In fact, he could recall touching almost every piece of wood and every nail. Maybe that was why, even now, he was more comfortable in the common room than his own bed. Still, no part of him believed Danni would feel the same.

It was Mother Superior's implication that bothered him.

"I'm dropping this off and heading to sleep myself," he said firmly.

She surveyed him with quiet suspicion for a moment and finally relented with a soft nod.

"God be with you."

"And with you."

Michael tapped lightly on the door. "You decent?"

"Not for several years now," she mumbled. "Go away."

"I have food."

"Fine. Come in."

He let the large tray enter the room ahead of him.

"Fruit, bread, cheese, some leftover mystery meat. I looked into the foil, but not too close."

Danni snatched an orange and leaned back against the headboard as she worked her thumb under the peel. She fed a slice into her cheek and spoke around it.

"At some point you're going to have to tell me how you got on a first-name basis with a Baron."

He grabbed a hunk of bread and then slid down to the floor, using the bed as a backrest.

"Not that much to tell. I made a mistake, and he made it go away."

Danni motioned for him to continue.

He sighed. "Growing up I got into some trouble. Family wasn't very family-like. LaCroix was the one who brought me here to Mt. Carmel. Just some guy doing me a favor. Seemed the right choice to let him, and the sisters made it feel like home, so I decided to stick around."

Michael held her eyes for a long minute. "Danni, what happened tonight?"

She shook her head. "I honestly don't know. Whatever that box was, I think you opened it."

It certainly seemed to make sense.

"And the things in it?" he asked.

Her voice was tired and soft. "Souls. And they were angry."

He closed his eyes and tried to call back what he'd felt in the cemetery. The breath-stealing rush of light and sound, like a heated wind off Bourbon street, as loud and raucous as the first night of Mardi Gras. It was awesome yet horrifying. He shuddered.

The questions began to surface faster than he could decide which answer mattered, so he asked them all.

"But how'd they get there? And now that they're out, where did they go? Did I cut them loose just to put them in limbo? That may not be a sin, but it sure doesn't fit into the vows, right? I mean, this wasn't something they covered in —"

Danni didn't answer. He looked up and saw why. In sleep, all the anger and coiled energy vanished. Her breathing was deep and even, her head tilted to one side. He watched for several minutes, as afraid to disturb her as he was transfixed. Soft lines replaced hard angles, smooth skin gleaming over long lines of muscle. Even as her body appeared to focus in on itself, her face turned outward, as if her closed eyes remained alert for any threat. She was like a panther at rest. A panther in New Orleans, vibrant and fearsome in the night. *Beautiful.*

Michael shook off the thought and stood. Carefully, quietly, he moved the tray to the floor and then reached one arm under her shoulders. He slid her down onto the bed with gentle prodding. When he started to move away, her hands wrapped around his forearm, her grip soft but not letting go. He swallowed hard and glanced back at the door.

Mother Superior's warning rushed back, and his stomach bottomed out. The feeling only seemed to worsen under the insistence of Danni's touch. Finally Michael slipped into bed beside her, leaned back against the headboard, and wrapped his free arm around her shoulder.

Eighteen

Sleep, *real sleep*, was more than a luxury. It was a goddamned miracle. So it was no surprise Danni's first thought as she woke was: *I must be dead.*

She lifted her head from the warm expanse of Michael's chest. His breathing was hushed in his own quiet slumber. Somewhere in the passing hours, her leg had come to rest around his, while his arm held her firmly against the hard line of his chest.

The sun broke through the blue-gray morning and warm sunlight lit his face. She felt his pulse beneath her hand, each rhythmic beat coursing in time with his soul. Gently, she traced the rough edge of his jaw up to the slick scar in his eyebrow. A man's history hid in his scars. A divot from a chicken pox, a thin line just beyond the edge of his hair line. Another, to the left of his jaw, jagged and deep at its inception. Her fingertips brushed his neck. Michael moaned pleasantly in response.

His eyes fluttered open and struggled to find focus on her face.

"Morning," she said.

"I, uh, you slept really hard. I was… any bad dreams?"

Danni searched her waking memory but came back blissfully empty.

"No. None." She looked down at their tangled legs. "I don't really remember how we got here, though."

Michael swallowed hard. He eased her hand away from his throat.

"It was a wild party. There was dancing, music, a couple of scary dudes staring each other down in a graveyard," he joked.

"I meant this."

She laid a firm hand over his chest to leaden the point. His heart slam against her palm, the first real indication she did anything to quicken his pulse.

Delicately, he began to unwind himself from her. "I was blathering on. Put you to sleep. It happens."

Danni followed him as he stood. He bent down and raised the tray between them.

"Apple? Another orange?"

She caught his hand, holding him in place as she searched his face. "Michael, I don't sleep. Not like that, anyway."

"Yeah. The Baron. Right. Maybe he can't in here? Anyway, you're awake now, and I need to go wash the graveyard off me." He motioned toward the narrow bathroom. "You probably should, too."

He was wrong. The Baron *could* find her here, he'd already proven that.

She watched Michael pull the door closed behind him and listened as his footsteps faded down the hall.

Maybe it's wasn't the place.

Father Clellan's voice droned up from the past.

"Long showers leave room for temptation, gentlemen."

His other favorite was: "Someone else needs the water you're wasting. Get clean and get out."

Clean. At least on the outside. Michael stared at his silhouette in the mirror. The eyes he didn't want to see were somewhere behind the steam. He jerked a towel from the stack beside the shower.

It's not like he'd sinned, unless lying to yourself was a sin. In that case, he was standing there sinning about his sins. He did the math on a Hail Mary as he finished toweling off. His hand paused over a cassock in the closet before sliding it aside for a pair jeans and a cotton dress shirt.

She was beautiful. That was no lie. And dangerous. No lie either. They needed her. That had the benefit of not being a lie while not quite being the truth. He tried again.

I need her. I...want her.

He buttoned the shirt and gave each sleeve a clean, single roll. Wanting her was as easy as breathing. Easier. But want *what*? That question was a rabbit hole and unfair for anyone to chase it too far. Anyway, there wasn't time.

Missing sisters, singing shadow men, trapped souls. It was like trying to solve a puzzle from the inside out. To be distracted by his desires now was unforgivable. Want could wait. Besides, there would be plenty of time to worry about that if they lived to talk about it.

Michael wiped the mirror to reveal his face. The eyes reflected there were clear. Conscience? Clear enough.

"Sufficient unto the day," he said to the mirror.

Nineteen

By the time Michael found her, Danni had powered through two pots of coffee and was pestering Sister Charlotte for a third.

"Come on, Sister. I've got a really long day ahead, and I don't want to collapse in the middle of it."

Sister Charlotte's scowl was fierce. "Young lady, I'm quite sure an elephant could cross the Sahara on less caffeine."

Danni clenched her fist around the Styrofoam cup. "Don't suppose you have a smoke, then, do you?"

The sister glanced side-to-side and then produced a long, thin cigar from her pocket. She offered it with one hand and put a thick forefinger to her lips. Danni nodded and wrapped her fingers around it.

"Now, now, Sister Charlotte," Michael said from behind her. "Lead them not into temptation."

Sister Charlotte blushed. "Of course. Forgive me—"

"No harm done, Sister," he said. "Surely they grow from the same earth as us, yes?"

He took the crushed Styrofoam cup from Danni's hands

and threw it away. "Ready to go?" he asked.

He didn't wait for the answer and paced off quickly. Danni caught up with him at the truck. The engine stumbled to life. Michael dropped the truck into gear before heading south into the Quarter.

They rode in silence. Michael leaned an elbow into the door and propped his head against his fist, drumming his free hand against the top of the steering wheel.

"So, want to tell me where we're headed?" she asked.

Michael guided the truck to the curb and killed the engine.

"No need. We're here."

Early in the morning, traffic was just a trickle of open-bed trucks hauling vegetables toward a shanty town of white, canvas tents. Michael tossed a quick wave toward the gathering crowd, before moving down an alley behind a restaurant. The blended scent of yeast and low country boil filled the narrow gap between the buildings.

The alley ended in a wider lot on the backside of another building. Michael took the steps up the back two at a time and then stopped at thick wooden door with a single square window. He rapped five beats against the frame, waited, and knocked again. A lock fell through the tumbler, and the door opened wide enough for Joto to glare at him.

His dreadlocks were the same smoky gray as his linen slacks, while his caftan seemed to have been woven from every color in a crayon box.

" 'Bout time you checked in," Joto grumbled.

Michael felt himself smile for the first time all morning. "How are you, Joto?"

"Better than you, comin' 'round at this hour."

Joto moved back and let the door swing open fully. His eyes widened on Danni. He jerked backwards, slamming the wheelchair into the wall.

"Tripping Jesus, Mike," Joto hissed. "A little warning would have been nice."

"You had to know we were coming sometime. Besides, you talked about her enough, I figured you wanted to meet her."

Joto turn and moved deeper into the building with Michael and Danni close behind him.

"I've talked about sharks, too. Doesn't mean I want to go surfing."

Joto glanced back at Danni, who responded with a big, toothy grin.

The floor transitioned from dingy tile to even fouler carpet as it opened into the shop. Sunlight leaked through bamboo blinds lowered over the street-side windows. The light caught long tendrils of earthy smoke as they floated up from a crucible at the edge of a rough-hewn table.

Danni's eyes wandered over the piles of paper and busted wares. She touched a chipped statue of Marie Laveau among the remnants of a half dozen take-out boxes and eyed Joto, wheel to nose.

"No altar. No icons. Racks of tourist crap," she said. "You give free hand-jobs with every purchase, or you make them pay for those?"

Joto sniffed at the insult, pushed himself up to a low table, and began sorting through a pile of dry herbs. "Nothing is free in N'awlins, but you already know that."

He closed his hand around a fistful of pink flowers before feeding them into the bowl. The flame leapt from inside and the white smoke turned pale red.

"What do you know about the toby at Bluesland?" she asked.

" 'Bout as much as you do."

"How'd you find it?"

"We have a mutual acquaintance." Joto used a long feather to stir the smoke into a vortex. His eyes reflected the shape of the cloud when he looked at her again. "A man at the Crossroads."

"Prove it," Danni spit.

"No."

Danni licked her top teeth. "No?"

She flattened her hands against the table and leaned into his face. Joto stayed still as her fingers fluttered above the pulse in his neck.

"You say you know the Baron," she said. "Then you must know what I'm capable of. Just one little trick. Nothing that will cost you."

Joto wet his lips but didn't take his eyes off her. "All right."

Raging veins and onyx pupils faded away until there was only the spiral of smoke. It moved counter-clockwise inside his eyes.

Dark laughter filled the shop. It rattled the shelves and the bottles stacked along them. Michael kept his eyes fixed on the reflection shifting in Joto's eyes as the sound swelled. It broke off with a bark of anger. Danni startled. Joto blink once and shook his head. When he looked up again, his bloodshot eyes were back in place.

"You're a *miroir*," Danni whispered.

"A what?" Michael asked.

"A mirror," Danni said. "A gateway to the Crossroads."

Joto went back to the mixture of herbs in front of him.

"The Baron said someone might be coming by looking for a champion. Said you were the one he wanted for the job." His face darkened. "As you can see, I'm in no position to deny him."

"Did he say why?" Danni asked. "He's got a hundred other people on the payroll that can do a lot more damage than I can."

"You sure 'bout that?" Joto flipped a cup over on the table and a fistful of small, dry bones clattered out in a loose pattern. "Ain't no one else I know carrying around a *lam te mouri*."

Danni's hand reached back to touch the top of her knife. She glared at Michael. "You showed him my *knife*?"

"You gave it *back* to her?" Joto asked him.

Michael winced and gave them both a slight shrug.

Joto turned his focus back to Danni. "After he showed it to me, I took the time to look it up. You bother to tell him what it does, or you just gonna let him figure that part out on his own?"

Danni started to answer, but Michael beat her to it. "You weren't exactly up front with me about why you sent me after her, Joto."

"Didn't see as it ran against your immediate goal," Joto said. "Then of course, that was before I realized something bigger was happening."

"Like a box of souls held up in Holy Cross Cemetery?" Danni asked. "That kind of bigger?"

Joto swept the bones back into the cup and added a brittle marigold head. "Made out of carved bone and sealed in human skin?" he asked.

Michael shuddered. "That was skin?"

Danni nodded. "Skin box. Sounds about right."

"Portmanteau," Joto corrected. "Who opened it?"

Danni tossed her thumb in Michael's direction.

"Good for you, Michael," Joto said. "Maybe that's why he chose you to play his side of the game."

"*His* side?"

"What game?" Danni asked.

When Joto turned the cup over on the table this time, the bones didn't fall. Instead, he caught a tiny harvest mouse in his palm. He let it run over his hands before releasing it on the floor. It darted forward, stopped, and then fled for a darker edge of the room.

"Some kind of bet between Samedi and LaCroix," Joto said. "Four portmanteaus, hidden throughout the city. Whoever releases the most, wins. And right now, it looks like LaCroix's ahead."

They sat with Joto's words for a long minute, considering each other quietly. Michael spoke first.

"These portmanteaus … they're all full of souls?" he asked.

Joto nodded. "Five hundred each."

As he did the math, Michael paled. "Where does somebody get two thousand souls?"

"The banshee witch," Joto said. "The demoness. That devil storm."

Joto began to work the smoke again, shaping it into a funnel before releasing it into the air. The cloud flattened out in places and expanded in others. Michael immediately recognized its shape.

"Katrina," he said.

Lightning flashed inside the swell. Michael smelled sea water and rust. Joto pushed back from the table and watched the storm build to encompass the ceiling as he spoke.

"Tools of man couldn't stop her. Magic couldn't either. But we tried."

The items on the table began to reorder themselves, small plastic bags stacked on jars, sticks forming arms. A dozen make-shift soldiers moved beneath the rising storm.

They cast fireworks into the base of the cloud. The lightning seemed to ease for a moment until the vapor took on a new shape, shifting out to a fat circle. It pulled everything from the tabletop directly into its center.

"The magic got twisted from our hands," Joto continued. "Thrown into the air with everything else before it crashed into New Orleans."

All at once, the cloud let go. The contents crashed loudly against the table. A few jars split, spilling a long line of dry poppy seeds and cloves across the floor. It startled Danni backwards and Michael to his feet.

"Two thousand people went missing in one day," Joto said. "Pulled up into the storm, lost to it. No saying what else got tied to it, or who."

The smoke began to dissipate as the sunlight ran it into the far edges of the room. Danni sank back against the wall and wrung her hands together.

"The Baron told me the same thing," she said quietly. "Katrina hit, magic got fucked up, and some of his got wrapped up in me."

Joto's eyes widened when she drew the knife from her back pocket, and stayed wide as she made a quick stroke against her palm. Blood welled to the surface of her skin.

She wadded the spit in her mouth, let it drop into the cut, and held it out for both of them to see.

"Apparently," she said, "manipulating flesh is something beholden to loa only."

Regardless of what he was supposed to be looking at, Michael felt his eyes drifting toward her face, to an expression that read of equal parts shame and fear.

The nail, the knife. Bluesland. Now this. How many more secrets did she have? Too many, he was sure. How many of those might get him killed, he couldn't decide.

What frightened him, however, was that he didn't care.

The wound stitched itself closed, and Joto blew out a long, slow breath. He pushed himself to the windows and pulled the cord to draw up the shade. The sudden light forced Michael to shade his eyes as they adjusted. Still, the warmth was cleansing and allowed him to take his first full breath in several minutes, only to have it stolen from his lungs when he found Danni's silhouette wrought in the fierce, white light.

Her body bent toward the sun, breast rising and falling as muscles flexed beneath her skin. Skin he could remember feeling as he held her against his chest.

Joto caught Michael's eyes and followed them to Danni. The line of his mouth hardened.

Danni stepped away from the window and back to the table.

"You said it was a bet," she said thoughtfully. "What's the prize?"

Joto kept a solid glare on Michael a moment longer and then spun to face her.

"N'awlins has always had a patron, head of household, so to speak. Sometimes it's Samedi, sometimes its LaCroix. Sometimes it's neither."

"What does that even mean?" Danni demanded.

"It means, whoever controls the souls, controls the Delta."

Joto crossed the shop to a tall armoire. He bypassed the baskets of raw roots and searched one drawer after another. Finally he returned with a card pinched between his index and middle finger. He handed it to Danni.

"You wanna know more, I suggest you start there."

"The Club Lakou," she read.

"It's a jazz club, a place where the Barons' entourage

can go to let their hair down. But it's neutral ground, so don't go startin' any shit."

Danni turned it over twice in her fingers. It was nothing more than a clear slip of vellum. No name. No number. "There's nothing on this."

"Take it outside." Joto motioned them to follow him again, and Michael realized he was herding them toward the back door. He opened it and held it for them.

"One other thing," Joto said. "Try to dress like you belong. Those outfits are more Goodwill than Good Times."

Danni tucked the card in her pocket, gave Joto a quick nod, and trotted down the stairs.

"Go on," Michael called after her. "I'll be right there."

She moved off down the alley without further debate. When he was sure she was out of earshot, Michael turned to Joto.

"You've been dealing with Samedi for a while now," he said. "You ever find anything to block him? Maybe hide yourself from him?"

Joto's eyes narrowed to slits. "Why you askin'?"

"Apparently he visits her in her dreams."

Joto rubbed a hand against his chin. "Yeah, he can get to me that way, too."

"So," Michael pressed. "You ever find a way?"

"Sure. Worked for about five minutes. Then he put me in the swamp and took my chair."

Michael patted Joto's shoulder. "Thanks anyway."

Joto caught his wrist before he started down the stairs.

"Michael, keep your eyes on your own ass, and off hers."

Twenty

"It's dangerous you know," she said as he slid into the truck. "To be indebted to one Baron while your best friend serves another."

Danni watched him from the corner of her eye. "I know how it's been working out for you and me. How does it work for you and Joto?"

Obviously not as well as he thought. Then again, Joto had always kept the details of his craft to himself. It wasn't until recently that those things begin to intersect with Michael's world.

"He's got his own agenda," Michael said finally. "But I've had his back, and he's had mine. Where our interests part, we'll say so."

"And when he has to choose between you and Samedi?"

"We don't put each other in that position."

Or maybe they did. Michael swallowed and kept his eyes on the road. It would have been easy to dismiss his growing suspicion if Joto had only suggested he seek Danni out. In retrospect, he'd done a great deal more than that.

For all Michael knew, every subtle hint handed off as back-alley rumor had come from Samedi himself. The longer he thought about it, the angrier he got. It made him bold.

"Your knife," he asked. "What's it do?"

When she didn't answer immediately, he pushed harder. "I think I have a right to know, seeing as I used it yesterday. Should I expect some kind of backlash?"

Danni shook her head. "No. It won't hurt you. Only me if I lose it again."

Impatient, he motioned for her to continue. Danni sighed.

"The Baron gave it to me so I can sever living souls from their owners."

"I'm sorry ... *what?*"

"That's what I do, Michael. I'm his ... " She let the thought die.

The heat rose in his cheeks. A single word lifted from the back of his throat in a growl. "Thief."

"And now you know," she said.

She turned the vellum card over in her hand and leaned toward the dashboard. "Still doesn't help us figure out where the hell this place is."

Sunlight filtered through the thin film. Sharp arabesques formed a semi-circle over her heart, longer, thinner lines splitting over her shoulder and well past her arm. A pattern cut in shadow, but its message unclear.

"What the fuck?" she said.

Michael tossed a few glances her direction, veering dangerously close to oncoming traffic. "Grab that city map in glove box."

Blindly, she patted around in the glove compartment until she found a folded map. She followed his thoughts and held the card in one hand as she spread the map open across her chest.

"There. Where's that green one hit now?" he asked.

Danni pressed a finger to the map to secure the point before pulling it away from her chest.

"Lakeview. Just north of the golf course," she groaned.

"Something wrong with that?"

"Just that Joto's right. You're gonna need an outfit that doesn't scream, 'I'm here to trim your hedges.' "

"I can blend. Can you?"

She stared down at her outfit and shrugged. "I've done all right with a lot less."

His neck was still hot with anger as he wedged his arm into the gap behind the seat. He pulled out a long, narrow box and dumped it into her lap.

"I asked Victoria to send it over," he said. "Didn't think you'd get to wear it so soon, though."

"What is this?"

"Just … open it."

Her soft gasp became his name as she pulled back the lid.

"Michael … "

She lifted the red dress from the tissue and ran her hands across the fabric. He kept his eyes on the road as she folded it back into the box and reseated the lid.

They rode in silence a little longer, but he could feel her eyes on him.

"So, I know why the Baron Samedi chose me," she began. "Any clue why LaCroix picked you?"

"Overdeveloped sense of irony." He turned left onto a one way. "It's bad enough the things Samedi has you do in his debt. LaCroix just likes to remind me *why* I'm in his…"

She considered him silently. His eyes stayed on the road, but his thoughts traveled beyond the blur of passing buildings.

"I had this Uncle Wayne," he said. "Used to play that 'got your nose' game with me until I started having nightmares. In my dreams, he'd be standing over me. 'Got your nose, Mikey! I got your nose!' And I'd look and he did. I'd wake up because I couldn't breathe."

He made another left. "Thing is, Uncle Wayne wasn't really Uncle Wayne. He was Uncle Wayne for a week or so, then there was also Uncle Jim, Uncle Dick … Cousin Kevin. Get what I mean?"

Danni nodded and Michael continued.

"My mom did what she had to do. We didn't have a phone, barely had an address. Joey and I didn't make it any easier on her. What kid running the streets in N'awlins would. When I was fourteen, Joey turned twelve. We celebrated by boosting a car. It was this really sweet Riviera. It was about five in the afternoon, and just off the business district. Perfect place for an idiot kid to take his first driving lesson, right?

"I was doing okay until I went the wrong way on a one-way. I freaked, slammed the gas instead of the brakes, and jammed it into a crowd of people. All I saw was black, white, black, white … "

Michael stopped at a red light, waited for it to change, and then signaled another left. "The cops put us in a holding cell while they tried to find our mom. About an hour later, they put a drunk in the cell across from us.

"He looked at me and said, 'Hey kid, what's black and white and red all over? A Buick.' He laughed until he choked. Had no clue it was LaCroix at the time. He asked me what I'd do to get out of all of it. Seemed natural to say anything."

Michael steered the truck through another left turn.

"From that point on, when the cops asked, Joey said he was the one driving. When the judge asked? When mom asked? Every time. Joey said he was driving. That it was all his idea."

Michael made another left.

"He was too young for prison, so he went to reform school. Supposed to be a place to teach young men the error of their ways, give them a trade. About a year in, he got in some fight with some kid who learned how to make a knife out a tooth brush. Joey died there.

"Right after that, I saw LaCroix again. Didn't want anything, just stopped by to let me know he took care of Joey. Reminded me I still owed him. Been that way ever since, I guess."

At the end of the block, Michael flipped the signal and cruised through the green light.

"You're going in circles, you know?" Danni said finally.

"Yeah, I think that's what LaCroix is trying to tell me, too."

Twenty-One

Cafe Del Sol encompassed a corner of The Quarter on contrary time with the rest of the world. Supper started at 5 a.m. and rolled into breakfast by late afternoon. When Danni and Michael arrived, second supper was in full swing. Michael snagged a small table outside and waved at a young black man in black slacks and a white button-down.

Danni sat, but kept her hands folded over the menu. "I don't feel much like eating."

"I get that," he said softly. "But we both skipped breakfast and I need a minute to process all of this before the next thing that tries to take my head off."

That much she understood. The tension was palpable. For him, it had resolved to carefully chosen, soft-spoken words, while all Danni wanted to do was pick a fight. With anyone.

The waiter set out a fresh pot of coffee and two mugs, a house standard she assumed, since they hadn't ordered it. Michael pointed to a few options on the menu and the waiter hurried away.

Michael laced his hands together and considered Danni. "What *is* the Crossroads, exactly? Hell?"

"In a manner of speaking," she said. "For Samedi, souls are power. The more he has, the stronger he is. At least, it seems that way."

"Seems?"

"None of this came with an instruction manual, Michael!" Her raised voice pulled the attention of several diners. Quieter, she said, "Joto seems to understand it better than I do. Why don't you ask him?"

Michael pulled in a deep breath and secured himself before asking the next question. "Is there *any way* to release them?"

"Sure. Toss in two pennies, call their name … *poof*! Free."

"Sounds simple enough."

Danni scoffed. "If you don't mind Samedi trying to kill you in the process."

"But … as long as there's someone on this side to revive you, you can come back, right?"

Her attention surfed out to the street. "To be honest, I wasn't sure that was actually going to work. I mean, CPR isn't the tried and true method of most people practicing voodoo."

"What is?"

"Don't go to the Crossroads." She heaved a sigh and idly swirled her coffee. "There are thousands of people in this city who would jump at the chance to set someone free, but less than a handful who would actually try. But I get it. Can you imagine letting someone you love spend eternity with Samedi?"

It was Michael's turn to look away and inspect the crowd of strange faces. Could he imagine? Was he already?

Danni voice softened a bit. "I wish I'd known about Gabriel at the time."

Michael tipped his head, thoughtful. "Would you have saved him?"

"Of course I would have," she snarled. "I'm not *proud* of condemning a bunch of innocent children to the scariest goddamn thing I've ever met."

"Only adults, right?"

Her eyes narrowed to slits. "You know, I was willing to take a lot of this from you yesterday, but it's a little hypocritical now. Speaking of which, did you ever tell anyone the truth about your little brother?"

It hurt less to hear than he thought it would, but it still stung.

"I've confessed it a few hundred times over the years, if that's what you're asking. But as far as telling someone who mattered?" Michael stared into his coffee, watching the cream cloud up to the surface before seeking Danni's intense, blue eyes again. "No."

"Then I guess that makes us both assholes, doesn't it?"

Michael chuckled grimly. "I guess it does."

She sat back and let her mind wander over the crowd.

Finally, Michael asked, "What about you?"

"What *about* me?"

"Tossing pennies into the Crossroads, calling your name. Would it work for you?"

"My thing's a little more complicated than that, I'm afraid." She touched the center of her chest to exaggerate the point. "Besides, I told you, that deal is done."

"Ever considered a new deal?"

The air between them shifted with the question. Her anger washed out under the tender weight of his eyes. She found herself floundering for a clear response. Had she considered it? Many times. It seemed every passing hour brought a new urgency and depth to exactly what she felt when she considered what her freedom would cost him.

The waiter returned with an armload of steaming dishes and arranged them on the table with deft skill. The scents hit her and she was suddenly starving and thankful to escape the conversation altogether. They ate in silence. Danni moved from one plate to the next, on a mission, while Michael seemed more interested in watching her.

By the time they finished, she was uncomfortably full. She stood and stretched while Michael settled up the bill. She crossed the street ahead of him. He rejoined her on the other side.

"If I find a way to release you from him," Michael told her over the top of the truck, "you know I'm going to take it."

Danni gave him a dubious smile. "I know now that you'll try."

Twenty-Two

"May we come in?" Michael asked. "We need your help."

Sister Ned unlatched the screen door and held it open. "Well, help is still in the job description, so I suppose that'd be the Christian thing to do."

The living room was lit only by what the afternoon sun could reach. Danni moved abreast of Michael and then stopped in the center of the room.

"Where's Gabriel?" she asked.

"Washing my back windows," Sister Ned said. "Good afternoon to you, too."

Danni moved toward the kitchen, leaving Michael and Sister Ned to exchange exasperated looks before trotting after her.

"Wound a little tight, isn't she?" Sister Ned asked.

"We've had an interesting morning."

A sudsy bucket and sponge lie forgotten by the back door. Gabriel sat on the tabletop with stars in his golden eyes. Danni leaned forward and pressed her hands down on either side of him.

"Where'd you get the ink?" she asked.

Gabriel ducked his face low and sucked a fat lip between his teeth. "I can't say."

Sister Ned's voice was soft but demanding. "*Gabriel.*"

"He made me promise I wouldn't say, Sister."

"I'm sure you can tell Danni," Michael suggested.

The boy considered it for a moment, tipping his head this way and that. But when he opened his mouth, Danni put up a fast hand to stop him.

"Wait!" She turned to Michael. "If he made a deal with the Baron and he breaks it, I may never be able to get him out."

She pulled in a long breath and looked at Gabriel again. "What *exactly* did you promise him?"

Gabriel's eyes dove between them again, but this time to where his shoes. Pristine white high tops with laces the color of sunflowers. He knocked his toes together.

"He said I could be the fastest. Said he'd give me the shoes, s'long as I didn't say where I got the ... " Gabriel tapped the side of his neck.

Danni guided Gabriel's face to the side and studied the bluish ink etched into his skin. Two long lines intersected at a T, and below it, a half-circle with its open side pointed down. Two more circles surrounded it all, a wheel within a wheel. Finally, she stepped back and sighed.

"Gabriel, shoes can be replaced," Sister Ned reminded.

"Feet can't," Danni countered. "If the Baron promised to make him the fastest, breaking the deal would give him every reason to go the opposite direction."

"And make him the slowest," Michael finished for her.

Sister Ned searched his face for further explanation, perhaps even his role in such a thing, but Michael only shook his head.

Gabriel pushed himself off the table as his soft smile spread to a full-blown grin. "He didn't say I couldn't show you."

/

Danni lifted Gabriel into the cab of the truck.

"We'll have him back before supper, Sister Ned," Michael assured her.

"You'd better have him back to finish my windows."

Michael nodded once and lurched the truck off down the street.

Half a block later, Gabriel had scooted himself away from Michael to snuggle into the crux of Danni's elbow. She guided Gabriel's chin up.

"Promise me you won't make deals like this with anyone else," she said.

"Why not?"

"Because while it might have seemed like a good idea, this man doesn't have your best interest at heart."

"I only see him in my dreams. He's always dancing and singing. It's always fun." Gabriel's face erupted in a grin. "You're there, too, sometimes."

Danni turned her face to the window.

Michael prompted Gabriel for directions, which he provided the way only a child can.

"Up by the bandstand where the man makes balloons. Yeah, there. Then by the … "

He guided them up Bienville to Rampart and then along the back of Congo Square. When they reached Toulouse, Gabriel seemed confused.

"I can't remember. I thought it was here but … "

"Oh, that's just wonderful," Danni grumbled.

Michael shot her a hard glare. "Just give him a second.

I'm sure he'll remember."

"No. He won't." She ran her fingers through her hair and adjusted in the seat to look at both of them. "Michael, I took you somewhere the other day to get a bottle of rum. Do you remember where it was?"

"Yeah, it—" He stopped, thought about it, and opened his mouth again. "It was …"

"Same Day," she reminded.

"Where?" Michael shook his head. It didn't seem right.

"I told you not to talk when we were in there. Make a left at the next light."

He followed her circuitous route back to Bourbon Street and parked at the curb. She lifted Gabriel out of the truck and they started down the sidewalk.

"It's a *deja vu* curse," she explained. "It locks on to the sound of your voice, because, well, who doesn't talk in a bar? Thus, when you leave, you forget you were ever there, until you stumble on it again."

Danni stopped on the banquette outside the narrow, glass doors. "Three hundred years, still the Same Day."

Michael surveyed the red-letter awning and as much of the interior as he could make out through the glare. Seemed familiar.

"This might be it," Gabriel said slowly.

"This is it." Danni turned to Michael. "Last time we were here, Carin told me he was paid up. I knew the minute I smelled it he'd made the paint for the toby. The same one that this little guy went back to Bluesland to paint. Right, Gabriel?"

Gabriel hung his head. "I'm not supposed to tell about that either."

"It's okay. I figured it out on my own." Danni stepped toward the alley and looked back at Michael. "Go in. Tell the bartender you're looking to get a tattoo. I'll see you in a minute."

Michael nodded and she jogged away. Gabriel started after her, but Michael stopped him.

"Come on. She'll catch up to us."

A cluster of bells jingled above the door as he pushed it open. The top rail hoisted liquors in a variety of shades. A string of Christmas lights lit up the rafter dust. It was all on the edge of familiar. Deja... right.

The bartender stepped out from the corner of the long bar. "Buyin', sellin', inkin' or drinkin'?"

"Inking," he said.

She waved him toward a curtain that divided the front from the back. He held Gabriel's hand tightly, making the extra effort to also keep him close. He worked his way through a crush of bodies. Tourists, college kids. A few wharf men throwing back tall flutes of something strong.

The curtain led into a shotgun kitchen. A thin man sat on a table, working a needle into the tip of a tattoo gun. He didn't look up when he spoke.

"Thirty for an arm, forty for a leg. Any other parts are negotiable."

Michael lifted Gabriel up by the hand. "Not got much meat on him, but what'dya give me for a whole ten-year-old?"

Gabriel giggled. The man's head shot up from his lap. "*Shit!*"

He shoved himself away from the table and made a quick turn toward the back door. An arm shot out and caught him beneath the chin. He crumpled, gasping and spitting.

Danni stepped away from the wall. "Hello, Carin."

Her fist landed against his face with a wet *pop*! The first wave of blood gushed from his nose.

Carin's voice was rasped but angry. "*Si to envie gagne bon vin soos mo gogot.*"

Another sharp jab to the face reeled him back against the Terracotta tile.

"There's a child in the room," Danni said. "Remember *that* kid?"

She forced his head back against the floor. Wild eyes raced between Michael and Gabriel. Danni pressed a boot against the top of Carin's hand.

"It's going to be pretty hard to draw with broken fingers," she warned.

"He said I'd be all paid up!" Carin cried.

Something creaked in the back of her throat. "How?"

"What I do! Mark the *bébés* on the neck!"

"How many of them?"

"I don't—"

Danni's boot ground down against his hand.

"Thirty! Maybe forty! Said he was just making sure his brother knew them kids was his!"

"Tell me something I don't know." She leaned her weight against his hand. "I'll stop when you do."

"I don't know! I said I thought he don't do kids. He got pissed. Blinded me for a week. I can't see, I can't work. So when my sight came back, I did what he say. Said he'd free me up if I kept quiet. I don't tell nobody. 'Dey came in. I inked 'em. Same mark. Every time." A painful noise ripped from his throat. "I don't know nothin' else!"

"What does it mean?" Michael asked quietly.

Danni tipped her head at Michael, nodded, and

refocused on Carin.

"Don't matter what it means, Cap. Dey just bait. It's the nuns that thing wants."

Michael stepped forward. "What thing? Where are they?"

High-pitch laughter rang through Carin's mouth like a siren winding up to a squall. Danni pulled her fist back again but stopped to lift her nose to the air. Rotten eggs? She could hear the faint hiss of air escaping a vacuum over the din of bar. She followed Carin's gaze to the stove.

"Uh, oh," he wheezed. "Mama's home."

Danni grabbed Michael and Gabriel, bringing them down to the floor as an orange fireball erupted over their heads. She pushed Gabriel out ahead of them. She tried to warn Michael to stay close, but her voice was lost under the roar of open flames. They army-crawled toward the curtain, but once they were standing again, Gabriel was gone.

"Find him," Danni commanded.

Michael went left while she went right. Any open space was suddenly occupied by a drunken tourist. The deeper she moved, the more the crowd swelled.

Danni was six paces down the bar when she realized she couldn't see the door, a wall, or Michael. The mortal crush of bodies expanded in all directions. She climbed onto the bar and cupped her hands to her mouth.

"*Michael!*"

The patrons whooped and chanted back. "*Mich-ael Mich-ael!*"

She spotted him buried in a cluster of men twice his height. He fought his way over their shoulders, and though she couldn't hear him, she saw her name on his lips.

A ribbon of sharp yellow flashed on a backdrop of darker hues. A splash of color, there and gone. Then there again. It took a second longer for her to place where she had seen it before.

Gabriel's sneakers. He zipped back and forth across the crowd, painting a straight path toward the door.

Danni raised her hand and pointed, but Michael only shook his head, confused. The crowd continued to chant below her. This was Mama Lou's magic. The only way around it was using it against her.

"Yellow!" she bellowed at the crowd.

They chanted back. "*Yell-ow! Yell-ow!*"

The words sang in. Michael followed Danni's finger to the bright yellow streak. Danni caught Michael's wave of recognition before she threw herself onto the crowd.

A hundred hands carried her along. Her boots pushed off shoulders and heads, twisting and tumbling as she follow Gabriel's sneakers to the front of the bar.

Michael was already there, holding Gabriel under one arm. He helped her down to the floor. Together, they threw their weight into the door and stumbled into the street.

The noise of the crowd vanished but her ears continued to ring. Danni gulped fresh air and turned to find Michael doing the same. Gabriel was leaning coolly against the lamp post.

She scooped him up and swung him around the street. He let out a squeal of unrestrained delight.

"You brilliant boy! Absolutely brilliant!" She set him back to the sidewalk but didn't release his hand. "What do you want? Ice cream? Pralines? Name it. It's yours."

Michael caught Gabriel's other hand and laced their fingers together. "Fastest boy in the world," he said.

They made their way back to the truck, laughing and swinging Gabriel between them.

Twenty-Three

"I look like a hooker."

Danni did a slow pirouette in front of the old mirror outside Mother Superior's office while Sister Mary Claire kept lookout. The red dress was more form-fitting than tight, but left absolutely nothing to the imagination. Danni tugged at the skirt hem and then decided it wasn't going much farther down her thigh, nor was there anywhere to hide her knife. She resigned to slipping it down the front, between her breasts, and said a silent prayer her cleavage would keep it in place.

"It certainly is…" Mary Claire eyed her, seeming to search for the right word. " …revealing."

Danni pulled her hair up from the back of her neck and then released it. "Make up?"

Mary Claire pulled a single tube of lipstick from her habit. She rolled it down the hallway to Danni. "It's all I could find."

The bottom said "Dark Side" but it was just a deep shade of plum. Danni ran it over her lips, recapped the tube, and rolled it back to Mary Claire.

"I need to get out of here before someone sees me in this." Danni gave herself one last parting look. "And by someone, I mean Mother Superior."

Mary Claire's wide-eyed nod was swift. She pulled an apple from the same pocket as the lipstick, but this time she met Danni at the mirror. "I found a red one. Why does it have to be red?"

Danni bit off a hunk and tucked it in her cheek. "Tastes better."

A dry voice filled the hallway behind them. "It's also helpful if you're looking to start trouble."

Mary Claire's smile flash-burned to dread. Danni swallowed hard, and the chunk of apple scraped painfully down her throat. Mother Superior tipped her head in the reflection of the mirror. Mary Claire didn't even excuse herself before heading back to the common room.

Danni wagged a finger at Mother Superior's reflection.

"You know an awful lot about voodoo for a Catholic," she said.

Mother Superior smiled, but the look was painful. "The goddess Eris used an apple inscribed with the words 'to the fairest' to start the Trojan War. Snow White's apple was full of poison. And then, of course..." Her eyes ran a slow path from head to toe before stopping on Danni's face. "There was Eve."

Danni bit down on the apple and tore off a fresh white piece of flesh. She snapped it greedily between her teeth and started down the hallway in the opposite direction. She let the ceiling carry her voice back.

"God is my judge, Sister. Not you."

The late-day sun baked heat off the back end of the kitchen entrance. A cluster of crows squawked and darted from the Dumpster as Danni hurried across the lot. Two blocks up and one over, a parking garage was emptying for the day. She snapped off another bite of the apple but spit it toward a trash can as she stepped onto the curb.

The security guard in the box gave her a fleeting look and then a longer one when she leaned into the narrow slot beneath his window.

"I did a dumb thing," she said.

"Did ya, now?" He rose from his seat. "What'd ya do?"

She bit her bottom lip. "Forgot my I.D." Her eyes darted toward the key panel. "Purse didn't match the outfit, and silly me, I need my car or I'm going to be late."

"Whoever he is, he's a lucky guy." The guard's hand slipped to the underside of the desk, and a second later the pedestrian gate opened with a rattling buzz. She started toward it, then stopped and held up the apple.

"Last bite's yours, if you want it."

The apple fit cleanly in the space beneath the window. He made a show of finishing it to the raw core and then spoke around the bulge in his cheek. "S'sweet."

Danni hustled inside the garage and followed the stairs up a few levels until she found one mostly devoid of foot traffic. She moved cleanly between the barriers, eyeing the cars as she went. She needed something sleek but low profile. Preferably fast. She settled on a Mercedes, mostly because it was unlocked and the key was in the visor. *Mostly*.

The ignition turned over, whispering only mild discontent as she gunned the engine to clear the lines. The smell of upholstery cleaner wafted from the vents, but it also held hints of expensive cologne. She flexed her hands to white knuckles around the wheel and spotted a pair of sunglasses in the center console. They slid over her eyes and cast the world in a purplish haze.

When she pulled from beneath the garage overhang, the sun was slipping fast toward the horizon. The tops of the buildings were wrought in a fierce, orange light that sent long shadows over the street. She merged into traffic, ducking in and out of the narrow gaps between cars with liquid ease.

/

Sister Charlotte stood with Michael on the steps of the convent with a cigarette cupped inside her hand.

"Mother Superior said she'll be praying for you tonight."

"Mother Superior is a wise woman," Michael answered.

"Didn't say why, though, just that – *oh*."

A sleek, silver Mercedes eased to the curb. The passenger-side window slid into the door. Danni leaned over the console, pushed the sunglasses down the bridge of her nose, and let out a low whistle.

"Well, well. You do clean up nice. Ready to take me dancin'?"

His hands fidgeted inside the pockets of simple tuxedo slacks. Danni popped the handle and pushed the door out to him. He slid into the passenger seat and closed the door.

"Don't wait up, Sister," Danni called.

He watched Sister Charlotte cross herself as they pulled away.

Michael's voice felt tight. "You look …"

Incredible. Beautiful. *Enticing*. Every time he started to say the words, they lost sound.

The dress sat in sharp contrast to the paleness of her skin. The red satin hugged the curves of her hips but left the full contour of her back fully exposed. His eyes were drawn to that exact spot as his better judgment fought his darker imagination for control.

Michael coughed hard into his fist. "Well, no one will be looking at me. Do you know where you're—"

The engine roared up the on ramp, slinging them into traffic with mere feet of clearance as they moved toward Lakeside proper. Just off the next exit, Spanish-tile roofs rose at competing heights. New-old cobble stone streets, Range Rovers in every driveway.

Danni ignored most of the stop signs, rolled the few she couldn't, and wound through the suburbanite landscape fast enough to turn it into a blur in his periphery.

"Uh, that was a … " Michael said as a red light whizzed by overhead.

"Never mind. You still have the card, right?"

Her answer was to fold up the edge of the dress where the card sat flush against her bare skin.

"No pockets," she said.

Michael swallowed hard, picked a spot in the distance, and focused on it.

"Yeah. Don't you just hate that?"

Danni tipped her head back and laughed. It spilled out in something rich and throaty, and filled the car. Michael caught himself grinning. Her hands were firm on the wheel, shoulders and arms parallel to the floor, confidence and joy wrapped up in every motion.

"This is much better than the carousel," he said under his breath.

And so much more dangerous.

Twenty-Four

"Should be right…"

Danni guided the Mercedes down a long expanse of tar pavement at the side of a warehouse. They coasted down a row of Cadillacs and high-dollar imports until she yanked the wheel, tapped the brakes once, and came to a perfect stop in a narrow space. "Here."

"Can I see the card, please?" Michael asked.

He didn't watch as she extracted it from its place against her thigh, keeping his eyes on the side of the brick building in front of them instead.

Michael held it up to the moonlight. The symbol stood out on the translucent vellum, perfectly superimposed on the brick wall.

"Subtle." He opened the car door but stopped before getting out. "You think we should lock it?"

"Do you think it would matter?" she asked.

The street-facing side of the building was nothing but high, windowless wall, same with the parking side. Just a cube of block and mortar the same deep crimson as dried blood overlooking the dark, rolling hills of Lakeside Golf

Course.

Michael followed Danni through the lot as she kept to the wall.

"Seems pretty quiet," Michael said. "Shouldn't we hear music, some thumping bass? Something?"

"I have no doubt we'll see and hear everything they want us to see and hear, until we don't," she said.

"Comforting, thanks."

At the back corner of the building, a wide shadow became an even wider man in a form-fitting tux. Michael could make out the matching spats covering the spit-shined shoes. A soft, low voice drifted from him, but Michael wasn't sure he'd actually spoke.

"Welcome to the Club Lakou."

"Thanks," Michael said. "We're uh… we're meeting friends."

"How fortunate for you."

This time, he was certain the guy's lips hadn't moved. The doorman stepped aside to let them pass.

They rounded the corner and the wall was gone, completely washed from the landscape. Alabaster stairs ran up to a landing just beyond his sight. Ebony columns supported more dark wood in the high ceiling. Spaced evenly between them, polished brass rods held fan blades that spun redolently in the night air.

The night air… *wait.*

Michael licked his top lip and spun around. The golf course was gone. Moonlight reflected on salt water in its place. He could see the ocean, hear the waves breaking against the shore.

"How is this possible?" he breathed. "The gulf is miles from here."

"It's a fade," Danni said. "Don't get lost in it, or you'll

never find your way out."

She turned him toward the stairs again. "Focus."

A hammered brass door frame surrounded a set of mahogany double doors, at the top of the stairs. Two more large men, identically detailed in tux and spats, flanked the door. They reached for the heavy brass handles in unison. The doors pulled wide, and the music Michael had expected overwhelmed him.

The tinkle of ivory keys. The long, slow slide of a brass trombone, topped by the trill of a satiny clarinet. The sound danced toward them on a wave of white smoke. It roiled over the threshold, bringing the scent of cardamom and lemon grass. It climbed around Danni's bare ankles like the barest kiss of mist off the open ocean, rich, briny and, more pointedly, *alive*.

The entrance stretched out into the main hall of black and white parquet. A maitre d' motioned them forward.

"This way, please."

Drumbeats marched them in. A tremolo on the rim of a snare, a light touch on a high-hat, and a pair of brushes on the tom toms. The kick beat felt a little flat to Michael but he lost interest as he eyed the timbered ceiling and the long miles of brass railing. Rows of tables ran up and around at varying riser heights. Each table was robed in dark fabrics and lit discretely from somewhere above.

A mahogany bar ran the full length of the room and disappeared where it curved off into the right side wall. The music came from somewhere beyond that. A spotlight burned a white halo at the top of the stage.

The drummer signaled the bridge. This time, the double tap on the kick drum's flatness matched the intensity of the brushes over the skins.

Small groups parted and couples shifted to one side or

another to watch Danni and Michael pass. The maitre d' led them down the middle of the room. He stopped at the edge of the dance floor and held a chair out, nodding to Danni.

"Madame?"

She took the offered seat, balancing gingerly on the edge as she locked her ankles together. Her eyes traveled to Michael, who stood beside her and gaped at the room.

She wove her fingers into Michael's, crushing the back of his hand as she yanked him toward the chair. He landed with a stuttered *oof*! Her mouth held just above his ear while her free hand marched a lazy rhythm against his collar.

"You should probably stop staring at the ceiling if you want to blend."

A blush burned his cheeks. So close to her, he could smell her skin and taste her breath moving against his skin. Michael turned his head, leaving his face inches from hers, his lips even closer.

"Is this better?" he asked.

Danni swallowed hard.

The maitre d' coughed, still waiting just off Michael's elbow.

"Drinks?"

Danni scanned the nearby tables and found other glasses full of amber and marigold poisons. Probably some house specialty.

"Two Makers Marks, four glasses," she said.

Michael waited until the waiter was out of earshot and then whispered, "Why four glasses?"

"Haven't you ever spit for your patron?"

"No."

She shook off her disbelief. "LaCroix must be more forgiving than Samedi."

When the waiter returned, Danni lifted her drink first. She flushed the first mouthful into the empty glass and felt the collective attention of the room unwind a half turn.

The spit-cup slid out to the edge of the table just as a smoky hand formed around it. She followed the line of his brocade jacket up to the rose pinned in his lapel. The Baron Samedi cocked his top hat, lifted the glass to his lips, and *glared* at Michael.

He kicked out his tails and spun a chair around to join their table. "He really is a dumb lummox, *non*?"

Danni spoke through gritted teeth. "*Akeyi yo.*"

"*Cher*. You're looking positively edible this evening." The Baron lipped the cigar and leaned in over his elbows.

"And you, *homme*? What have you to say to me?"

Before Michael could answer, Danni flattened her hand between them.

"Michael, don't. Baron. *Please.*"

Samedi held Michael's eyes for a moment longer, then flicked his chin at the dance floor. "Shall we, *cher*?"

He snapped once. The warm yellow light was replaced by a long, white spot haloed around their table. The swinging jazz beat shifted to a calypso rhythm. A white-gloved hand unfolded to her.

Though spoken as such, it wasn't a request.

Danni glanced at Michael. "Don't go anywhere."

The Baron's right hand curled around hers. He drew her out to the dance floor. The light followed them, shutting out the crowd as he paced off a wide circle around her. His steps fell into time with the snare drum as he hooked her against the line of his body.

"Quite the outfit," he purred. "I almost see a bit of the

old you in there."

"The *old* me?"

He swept two fingers against the soft skin below her ear. Where she should have felt skin, she only felt heat. The sensation settled into her chest before igniting the path down to the center of her thighs.

"That young, irrepressible ingénue fresh off the cell block. Answering the door before opportunity has a chance to ring the bell." He pulled in a long, hissing breath. "I am so fond of that girl."

"What do you want?" she asked.

He twisted her away, letting her find the beat before she worked back to him in three short ball steps.

"To give you a gift."

Unseen hands slid beneath her dress, taking their time to smooth the softer parts of her inner leg and secure something in place around the widest part of her thigh. Danni lolled her head against his shoulder. The Baron's withdraw was equally slow and teasing, moving up beneath the dress.

Though she couldn't see him clearly, she held her eyes in the direction of their table, squinting to find Michael's outline against the backdrop of the club. For the moment he was motionless, hands rested in his lap, watching along with everyone else in the room. She found herself wondering if Michael's hands felt the same.

The sensation snapped off and the Baron voice hissed against her ear. "Do you mean to insult me or anger me, *cher*?"

Danni laughter was low and dark. "You always did hate to be upstaged."

"I've *never* been upstaged," he growled.

He twirled her into a quick cross-body lead, exchanging

his position for hers and back again. The movement and the light stole her sense of direction, and she could no longer tell if Michael was to her left or right, forward or back.

"Now I have your full attention."

The Baron dipped her hard, jerking her spine ramrod straight. A hand worked its way up her thigh before changing directions as he whipped her upright again.

"Tell me you don't enjoy our little interludes."

She shifted against him, as much a part of the dance as an attempt to determine, by touch alone, what he'd affixed to her leg. Whatever it was, it was tight like a garter but smooth, like nylon.

"What is that?"

"Trust me, you'll need those."

"To find the next portmanteau?" she dared. When he didn't answer, she tried again. "That's what all this is about, isn't it? These boxes, the souls?"

The Baron's eyes were hard and unblinking. Her hands stayed in motion, spanning every inch of his jacket as she crossed around behind him. She lifted herself onto her tiptoes and whispered into his ear.

"Can't you just tell me where they are?"

He covered her hand with his, leading her back to the center of the light. "Just listen to the music, *cher*. Feel the beat."

If it was a clue, it made no sense. Still, she tried to push her focus beyond the dance to the music swelling to crescendo. Each deep thump and stuttered rhythm spoke a language of its own, but what it was saying, if anything, she couldn't tell.

"What happens if I can't find it?"

The Baron made a haughty noise, a cross between a laugh and a sneer. He twisted her in fluid movements, guiding their sway to the music's cadence until she was resting against his chest again.

"Makes no difference to me."

"Really?" she hissed. "Because by my count, LaCroix is five-hundred up."

That earned her a sharp jerk and turn. Her bare back landed against the iron expanse of his chest. He held her arms wide. Fingers formed beneath his shirt. She squirmed against the feel of them as they touched her spine, so many hands moving against her skin. They stabbed into the spaces between her ribs with breath-stealing intensity. The Baron held her there for four measures rest with his mouth pressed to her ear.

"That wasn't nice, *cher*."

"I'm sorry," she wheezed.

The fingers dug deeper. "Mean it."

"I'm sorry, Baron."

The fingers withdrew, but he gave her no time to catch her breath before sweeping her around to face him again. Amber light formed interlocking circlets in his eyes.

"Perhaps you should spend less time trying to fuck the boy, and more time trying to find my things."

"You sound worried," she said.

His dismissive laughter rose with the timbre of the bass line.

"He got lucky, but it won't last. Make no mistake, *cher*, he plays to his own ends."

"He's better than you know."

"Better than *you*, you mean." He twirled her, and each quick flash past his face showed an ever-widening smile. "Are you so certain?"

The Baron placed her back against him again. An arm slithered out around her, and he used his fingertip to cut a perfect circle in the curtain of light.

Michael was still at their table. But he was no longer alone.

Twenty-Five

"They look good together, hey?"

Michael startled. LaCroix looked back at him, amused. "What? You thought I wouldn't be here?"

Michael couldn't help but notice that LaCroix and Samedi were dressed almost identically from top hat to tails. The only difference was the deep purple flower at LaCroix's lapel. Michael followed his eyes back out to the dance floor.

"Look at the way her body bends to him, the way she follows his lead." LaCroix made a *tsk-tsk* sound. "Ooo, *oo*! My brother is treatin' himself right with that one."

"I'm going to kindly ask you to stop," Michael growled.

"Or what?" LaCroix cocked a hand against his thigh, more predatory than amused. "What you gonna do about it, *hero*?"

Samedi's hand was making a slow circuit around Danni's waist. Their movements were effortless, as if one was an extension of the other. What bothered Michael was that Danni seemed to be enjoying it.

"You can be jealous, Michael," LaCroix said, "but that's all you'll be. If he's a gator, she's his sharpest tooth."

LaCroix palmed one of the empty glasses on the table and pushed Michael's drink forward. Michael hesitated and then mouthed half the drink before flushing it into the empty glass.

"Now, there's a good son," LaCroix's said and vanished, taking the drink with him.

The song ended with wild applause as the crowd hooted Samedi's name. He dropped back from Danni in a low bow and then swept his arm up toward the ceiling and disappeared.

A new song started. Danni made the slow walk back to the table. Michael couldn't help but notice the painful hitch in her hips as they rocked toward him. Michael stared at the watery ends of his drink and then tossed it back as she slid into the seat beside him.

"LaCroix?" she asked.

"Gone for the moment." Michael cleared his throat. "Are you all right?"

"There's one here," she whispered. She made a quick sweep of the room, from the bar to the bandstand. "A portmanteau."

"Samedi told you that?"

Danni took a long, settling sip from her glass and shook her head. "Not exactly. Every time I asked, he avoided it. Just told me to listen to the music, to feel the beat."

The place was too big to search properly, and there was no guarantee they wouldn't be tossed out on their ass for trying.

"So, we listen to the music," Michael said. "That's not so hard. I've loved this stuff all my life. I've followed all the greats, from Troy Andrews back to King Oliver. It would have been great to have these seats if Pete Fountain played here. This place would have wailed. Or Buddy Guy? I mean, this band is good, but Buddy Guy? He'd have set this place on fire. Probably would have spent an hour tuning the drums first."

"That's great, Jazzman, but what are you *hearing*?"

Michael closed his eyes and let the music fill his head as the alcohol buzzed warmth into the back of his eyes.

"You hear that rasp?" Michael asked. "Every time the drummer kicks the bass. There. And there. He's probably been stomping it all week, put it out of tune."

Danni twisted toward the bandstand.

"There," Michael said again. He opened his eyes. "It sounds like he's kicking a brick."

Their eyes met.

Michael counted at least forty heads, another dozen waiters, and the musicians. They'd never make it to the stage unnoticed, let alone inside the drum.

"I need a pack of matches," Danni said.

Michael patted his pocket and found a white, foldout packet with red lettering that read: *Chautain Rue.*

She snapped them from his fingers. "Perfect."

Danni went to work bending the heads down and around the pack to meet the strike. She reordered them one by one as she kept a tight eye on the room.

"You think you can make it to the stage and back in the time it takes a match to burn?" she asked.

Michael checked the distance. "There's a lot of people in here, and the drummer looks like he might clobber me if I mess up his rig."

"They won't be looking at you."

She slipped her hand into the top of her dress. Michael's eyes widened as her hand returned with a fresh cut on the thumb.

"What the hell is in your … dress?" he asked.

She ignored him as she pinched the pad of her finger, working the blood to the surface.

"Close your eyes," she said. "When you hear me strike the match, open them and head for the stage."

He did as he was told. A seconds later he heard a *pop!* and smelled sulfur. The first thing he noticed was the silence. The music stopped. Conversation, too. Michael opened his eyes.

The dancers, the waiters, even Danni, were frozen in place. The only thing still moving was the flame in her hand.

Michael slid between couples, ducked under the extended arm of the maitre d', and almost fell into the horn player. He hustled around the edge of the bandstand and dropped to his knees behind the drum kit. He pushed aside the vellum front skin of the bass drum. The portmanteau sat in the middle, bathed in a warm glow.

Michael retraced his steps, weaving his way back across the dance floor. He sat down just as the fire in Danni's hand began to stutter. The flame reached the stiff cardboard at the strike plate and lost its energy, snuffing out in a light wisp of gray smoke. He tucked the portmanteau under the table.

Danni glanced at the burned matchbook in her hand and then at him.

"I got it," he whispered.

She started to stand. "Let's get the f—"

A hand clamped down on her shoulder, and a deep voice rattled down a tuxedoed arm. "Miss, you and your date best come with us."

Michael twisted around to find two suited giants

flanking them.

"We were just walking out," Danni said.

She tried to stand again, only to be slammed back down in the seat.

"Not necessary. We'll take you where you need to go."

They lifted her and Michael, chairs and all, up to shoulder level. The table crashed over on its side. Michael tried to shift out of the seat, but one meaty hand kept him in place as the other lifted him off the floor.

He tried to see Danni's face, but her back was to him, pinned to the parade end of the world.

Twenty-Six

The ride through the room was more than frightening. It was also embarrassing. Several people threw lit matches, while others spit at the floor. Some even reached for them as they passed. Hard fingernails dragged across Danni's ankles, and then lost grip when she was yanked past their reach.

"Some folks just can't take a joke," Danni mumbled.

They were marched down a winding staircase that, if Danni had to guess, took them well below ground. They were lowered roughly to the floor and then pushed forward down a steady slant. It dead-ended, and a handleless door slid sideways into the wall.

Another sharp shove staggered Danni into an arena. Railed walkways surrounded them on all four sides. A reddish glow rose from the open space along with enough heat and humidity to form a small layer of hazy mist over their heads. Where the floor wasn't dank, standing water, the sand had been combed into neat garden lines. Hunks of flesh squished under her feet, issuing a rotten-sweet perfume of blood, sweat, and bile that the humidity refused to send in any other direction but up.

The bodyguards moved past them to stand beside a man on the opposite end of the arena. Light bent off his bald head at low angles, giving his mulatto skin the same glossy sheen as his suit. He looked surprisingly confident for being swathed in purple silk. The tails of his jacket ran the full length of his legs which, gauged from a distance, put him a full head and shoulders above Michael.

Still, he wasn't the one dealing regular damage in this room. Divots in the wainscot walls reflected the repeated abuse of something much larger. Body-shaped patches had been repaired and painted with alternating shades of black matte and gloss.

Danni swallowed the quaver in her voice, tried to sound brave but settled on smug instead.

"Where *do* you find a lavender tuxedo?"

The man slid out an incredibly long leg, held his arms high, and postured for a moment. "It's heliotrope. Don't ya like it?"

"Not particularly."

Two coins snapped together in his fist. He took a small step forward, two full strides for Danni. White teeth ground down on the end of a toothpick, working the lines of sinew around his jaw. A charcoal tattoo spanned from forehead to neck. Instead of the traditional hint of ink worked into the skin, his had been gouged into long, puckered lines she was certain impacted the underlying bone.

"That looks like it hurt," she said.

Idly, he touched his temple and then swept down into an elaborate bow.

"Roben LeChance. Proprietor."

"Bonnie." She chucked a thumb over her shoulder at Michael. "Clyde. We were just leaving."

She heard the door slide shut behind her, locked by an unseen mechanism that sounded as solid as it did lethal.

Roben shook his head. "Only one way out this room. For either of you."

She tossed a panicked look at Michael. "He didn't do anything."

"What's the phrase they use? Guilt by association?" Roben's wheezing laughter sounded raw and vicious, like a blender full of babies. "'Sides, he's got somethin' I'll be needin' back."

Though she'd been painfully aware of its presence for several minutes, Danni would be damned if they were just going to hand him the portmanteau.

She staggered her feet in the sand and baited Roben with a curl of her fingers. "Come get it then."

His gaze shifted between her and Michael. "What'dya say we make it a trade. Keepsake for keepsake."

A hand slid deep into his pocket and returned with a fistful of beads. He lobbed them across the arena to Michael's feet. Danni's eyes picked over the strange knot before noticing a single loose end holding a crucifix.

Her eyes locked with Michael's as he fought to swallow the gag that rose in his throat. The first bit of true rage pulled a curtain of color across his cheeks.

His voice came out in a gas-line whisper. "Where are they?"

"Let's just say they won't be needin' those anymore." Roben brushed the coins together again. "But you might, in a minute. Hand over the box."

Michael's answer was resoundingly clear as he jammed the portmanteau securely inside his shirt and flexed his hands to fists.

"No bother," Roben said. "We'll pick it off your

corpse."

The two bodyguards moved to the corners and made quick but agile leaps over the lowest rail. Roben tapped the coins face to face, and the light changed. The haze lifted to reveal a crowd seated around the highest rail. At least a hundred people dressed in old-world finery stared down at Danni with blood lust in their eyes.

The reality sank around her, as sure and sticky as the fog lifting from the sand. Danni felt her stomach bottom out, chased by the last real promise that they'd make it out of this room with in one piece.

Her eyes narrowed on Roben. "I wouldn't do this if I were you."

"If you were me, darlin', you would'a liked my suit."

Roben spread his arms wide. A rumble echoed up from deeper inside the building. The crowd drew a collective gasp as glasses tinkled across the tables. The sand began to sag in the center of the arena, running out like an hourglass as a hole opened. More mist clouded up around them. Danni recognized the smell of burnt meat left rotting in the sun as a musk particular to water snakes.

She gripped the belt the Baron had placed around her thigh. Her fingers found the top of a slim knife and remembered the Baron's words. *You'll need those.*

Roben dusted stray lint from his collar. "S'matter? Ain't never seen a koulev?"

Loosely translated she knew it meant 'snake', but what slithered from the hole was something divergent of the term. It was a grotesque combination of man and animal, genderless upon immediate inspection. Its snout was short and wide, turned up like a viper but on a much more human face. A hood of thick cartilage connected at its brow line and fanned out around its head. The remainder of its body dumped from the hole, moving faster than anything its size ought to. Two yellow eyes settled on Danni as a forked tongue shot out hungrily from between black lips. Its mouth parted again, but this time the hiss became a scream.

Roben passed a coin over the back of his hand then narrowed his eyes on Michael. "Sisters be happy to see you again, I reckon."

Danni didn't miss the underlying fury in Michael's words or the heat of his breath as it passed over her neck. "What did you do to them?"

Roben smiled. "You have any idea what it takes to grow up one of these things?"

Danni's words came out slowly as she fought back the nausea she found in saying them. "You fed them to your snake?"

"Sure. Likes the holy ones the best."

Danni took a long, steady breath while she ran her eyes over every grotesque inch of the koulev. It bobbed beside Roben, twice as wide and three times as tall. Long, cream-colored scales expanded and contracted across its underbelly. If it had to breathe, it could be strangled. It wasn't much of an advantage, but it was something simple and clean her mind could wrap around.

Roben rose, suddenly weightless and floating. He kicked himself up behind the safety of the lowest rail, and then he began to sing.

"My gran'ma and your gran'ma were sittin' by the bayou … "

The koulev hissed and snapped again, its yellow eyes fixated on the coins rolling across Roben's knuckles. Michael made the connection at the same time Danni did.

"Think those are what controls it?" he whispered.

She nodded once. "I'll take the snake, you take Captain

Leisure Suit?"

There was cold fury in Michael's voice. "Deal."

Roben tossed one of the coins into the air. Danni's eyes followed it as it turned heads over tails. It hung at the top of its arc, spinning until its revolutions were so quick it became an edgeless ball of copper light. The koulev roared and swelled, cocking its head madly until it finally centered on her.

Without much thought to where they'd land, Danni tossed Michael right while she dove left. The koulev struck the ground between them, sending a swell of sand into the dim light. Danni used her momentum to roll behind a long coil. By the time she made it back to her feet, the koulev had found Michael.

Its forked-tongue shot out, tasting the air as it cambered back to strike. Michael fought himself backward, heels kicking wild sprays of sand as he failed to find his footing. The crowd roared above him as odds were hollered over the horrible, screaming hiss of the snake.

Danni pulled two short knives from the holster around her thigh. They weren't much, about the length of her hand, but they were sharp. She bit them between her teeth, kicked the heels from her feet, and ran barefoot up the koulev's spine. She made a screaming leap towards the back of its head. Her fingers wrenched down around thick braids of cartilage. She drove the first knife as deep as she could. The koulev reared and bucked, twisting away from Michael but taking her with it.

"Get the coins!" she screamed.

Michael scrambled to his feet. He couldn't make out much more than shapes through the mist, but Roben was the only lump of lavender in the place.

Michael stayed closed to the wall, narrowly avoiding the body of the koulev as it trashed across the sand. Something hard stuck his temple. White spots exploded in the corner of his eye, causing him to stagger into the wall. A thick-bottomed glass tumbled away from him. He looked up to the rail. The crowd spit and shouted at him, tossing their drinks down into the sand.

The koulev howled behind him. Its screams alternated between rage and pain in shrill bursts. All he could see of Danni was flashes of red satin as it whipped her wildly through the air.

His eyes searched for the ball of copper light suspended above the pit. He raced toward it again. His left foot kicked off the bottom of the wall as his right hammered him upward. Roben took a startled step back. Michael's feet found the upmost ledge as he swung over the rail.

A bodyguard moved to intercept him. Michael dropped to his knee, using the guard's own inertia to toss him easily over the rail. The guard landed in the sand pit.

Roben turned half of the coin over the top of his fingers. The koulev whirled toward them, but instead of striking, it lifted its tail and smashed the bodyguard into the sand. If there was any question as to how much of the thing Roben controlled, Michael now had the answer.

"What you gonna do now, lover boy?" Roben cackled.

The second bodyguard reached for him, but Michael pivoted back toward the rail. His extended an arm in front of him and leapt toward the coin, stretching as he felt his body begin to fall. His fingers closed around it and snatched it from the air.

Michael fell back into the pit, bounced, and rolled into the wall. He opened his fist and stared at the coin. It glittered with alternating ribbons of gold and copper, some amalgamation of metals melted and pressed to the size of a half-dollar. He shook it and then beat it against his hand. The koulev didn't stop.

Danni clung to its head. The koulev twirled and nipped its short mouth sideways, taking them both in tight circles. It whirled her past the crowd. They booed and spit and tossed drinks in her face. She fought for more leverage as she drove another blade closer to the top of the koulev's head.

It hissed and reared. Danni lost her grip. Michael sucked in a sharp breath as she half-fell, half-slid down its back. She landed hard, then rolled wide as the koulev came in for another blind strike. It smashed into the sand and left a two-foot indentation in its wake.

The pit was too small to fight something so big, Danni broke for the door they'd entered on, pulling its attention along with her.

"Come on, you fucking thing! Come get me!" she screamed.

The koulev chased her, piling its body to her left and right, leaving no room for escape. She pivoted and ran backwards until she was pinned against the door.

"Danni!" Michael yelled.

Roben waved his half of the coin, seeming to call the koulev back, but it didn't respond. It roared again and stuck.

Michael caught a flash of red as Danni dove under it, then heard the crunch of wood fracturing under pressure. The koulev jerked back again, and Michael saw the opening where the door had been.

The koulev's head spun one way while its body went another. The tail caught Danni squarely across the back of the knees and sent her into the wall. Her hands rose to break her fall, but her body took the majority of the impact. Michael saw her try to rise and crumple against the sand instead. The koulev dove down to her.

She grappled with its head. It snapped and spit in her face. Fangs the length and width of her arms craned out of its open mouth. She strained away from them, but its mouth only seemed to stretch wider. A fang connected with her cheek. She screamed and threw a sharp strike into its slitted yellow eye. It reared back, shaking its head, effectively blind.

Danni raced across the arena toward Michael, vaulting and sliding over the koulev's body as it moved to intercept her. She landed on her knees beside him. His hands wrenched down on her shoulder, as much to steady himself as assure him of her presence.

His voice broke around his words. "You're alive."

"Just barely," she panted. "We have to get to the door."

Danni reached down the front of her dress and withdrew the bone-handled blade. She tested its weight in her hands then yelled at the koulev.

"Hey! Over here!"

Its mouth unhinged in a scream. Danni over-armed the knife. It tumbled end over end and then sank into the back of the koulev's mouth. A fetid pulse of thick, black blood oozed from the newly opened flesh. The koulev bucked and howled, a sick sound erupting from its throat in wet floods of brackish blood. It slammed its face into the ground, each time making a wet slopping noise as it beat itself senseless.

The smugness melted from Roben's face, replaced quickly with fear. He stared at the other half of the coin in his hand, twisted around, and ran deeper into the club. Between his sudden exit and the realization that the odds had just changed in Danni and Michael's favor, the crowd began an equally panicked charge over each other and out of the room.

The koulev crashed into the rail, splintering tables and chairs as its jaws snapped down on anything it could find. Frantic screams were silenced by wet, gurgling crunches.

Danni grabbed Michael's arm. "Come on."

They ran through the door and up the hallway, hand in hand. The wall exploded behind them. The koulev's head tore through the opening, but its body did not, firmly trapped in the narrow doorway. Its screams chased them back toward the scented smoke and tingling jazz. The music snapped off. Several waiters and patrons stood, but made no move to stop them as they raced toward the entrance. Danni shouldered the heavy doors open ahead of Michael, ran down the alabaster stairs and into the parking lot.

She threw herself into the driver's seat of the Mercedes, but gasped when she spotted her reflection the rearview mirror. The koulev's venom had wasted no time disintegrating the meat of her cheek. Exposed bone glistened in the hollow below her eye.

She spit into her palm and massaged it into the wound as she turned to Michael and patted his chest for a similar injury.

"Did it get you anywhere?"

Michael searched his hands, his legs, and his chest. He touched the corner of his temple and found only a small amount of blood.

"No," he said. "I'm okay. But your face ... "

She checked the mirror. It was already healing. She keyed the ignition and doubled over the wheel in pain. Michael reached for her, but she waved him off.

"They'll heal," she grunted. "Bone takes longer than skin."

As they transitioned from blacktop to pavement, the Mercedes' engine turned into a thunderous sound like a zipper pulled across the sky. Danni blew every light and stop sign until they were back on the interstate.

Michael turned the coin over in the light of passing street lamps. The raised impression looked like a Vitruvian Man with his arms and legs held out at his sides. The reverse side was blank, as if whatever image belonged there had been stricken clean from the coin.

"How do you think it works?" he asked.

"No clue, but I know who we can ask."

"You sure you don't want to get cleaned up first?" he asked.

She shook her head and tucked the coin between the empty sheath and her bare thigh.

"It's a good bet Joto's already hearing about what just happened. Tonight we can ask. Tomorrow I might have to beat the answer out of him."

Twenty-Seven

By the time she pulled into the alley behind Joto's shop, Danni's breath had quickened to short, painful pants. Whatever wasn't covered with sand was soaked in something else. Koulev blood crusted in her nails, the creases of her knuckles, and between her toes. The venom had easily eaten through her satin dress and left violent burns on her collarbone.

Michael was certain she'd struck and broken every rib on her left side and maybe some on the right. He followed her careful steps as she negotiated the way up to the backdoor.

Danni hammered a fist against the frame. "Joto! Open the damn door!"

When he did, she pushed past him without invitation and moved deeper into the shop. Michael followed and reached for the first aid kit against the far wall. He unfolded it next to her as she slid onto the table, and tore open a fresh package of gauze.

Most of the damage was superficial, except her cheek, which had already healed to a deep bruise below her eye.

Still, she hissed when he passed the gauze against it.

Joto watched from the edge of the table. "You look like you went ten rounds with a—"

"Koulev." She chucked the coin at his chest. "Any idea what this thing does?"

Joto held it up to the light and pressed the fat pad of his thumb against the edge.

"*Vire-pyes.*" He flipped it back across the short distance. She caught it against her chest. "Half of one, anyway. It's a bonding mechanism, bends whatever creature is bound to it to the priest's will."

"Roben," Danni said.

Joto sniffed. "LaChance? Where'd you see his sorry ass?"

"Club Lakou. Where he tried to kill us."

Joto shook his head. "Always been a scary dude. Light matches just to see what they'd burn."

"Houngan?" Danni asked.

"Mount."

"Of course. The tattoo." Danni ran a hand over her mouth and then looked like she regretted it.

Michael reached for a fresh pack of gauze. "What's a mount?"

"Think groupie with a twist," Joto said. "Roben's Baron can hop in his skin whenever it wants."

"If Roben's a pony, who's his rider?" Danni asked.

Joto shrugged. "There's more than a few I can think of who'd jump on someone like him. He's all tied up in local real estate, built a nice fortune even without all the back-alley dealing he does. Owns *this* building, as a matter of fact, so do me a favor and don't be kicking at him too hard."

"He fed the nuns to his giant snake," Danni said around

gritted teeth.

"And I'd say you settled your score," Joto said. "It's no parlor trick, bringing up a creature like that. There's no way he can control it without both coins. Can't say his Baron's gonna be too pleased about that."

He made a fair point, one Michael was almost willing to accept. Danni's soft grip stilled his hand, and his eyes found hers. The intensity in her expression startled him. Sorrow, pain, but also a seriousness that said she would kill Roben if Michael asked.

"It's not my vengeance to take," Michael said finally. "As long as we stopped that... thing."

"Might not be that simple." Joto reached for one of the leather-bound books on the shelf beside the desk. He unfolded it in the cradle of his arm and turned it to face them both.

"Just because it's not killing for Roben, don't mean it ain't killing."

Age had bled the ink purple. The drawing of the koulev looked almost cartoonish beside a margin of text. Michael knew enough Haitian to recognize the words that mattered: *savage*, *violent*, and *wild*.

Danni pinched the bridge of her nose. "Guess leaving it to nature's not an option, huh?"

Joto chortled. "Nature? Hell. The National Guard wouldn't be able to put that thing down."

Michael reached inside his shirt and withdrew the portmanteau. It was surprisingly intact, considering what it had been through, but he felt a dull ache in his side where he'd landed on it at least once.

"At least we got what we went for."

It was similar to the one from the cemetery, almost identical, except for what he knew about it now. Michael ticked his fingernail against the corners, in the small gaps between vertebrae.

"May I?" Joto asked.

Michael passed it to him. Joto rolled it over in his hands, held it to his nose, and pulled in a deep breath.

"That's skin, alright." he said. "Skin somebody spent a lifetime takin' care of. So, who found it?"

"We did," Michael said quickly. "We figured it out together."

"Maybe so, but who put hands on it first?"

"He did," Danni said.

"Okay then," Joto said. "Technically, it's his to open."

Michael hesitated and gave Danni a sympathetic look. She just shook her head. "There's no sense in debating it. Go ahead."

Michael patted around Joto's table and found a small, pot metal knife with a voodoo doll handle. It slid into the top of the box easily. Michael squeezed his eyes shut, turned his head, and waited for the rush he'd felt in the cemetery.

Nothing happened. He wiggled the knife side to side. Still nothing.

"Wrong knife, *homme*," Joto said.

"Fuck," Danni said.

Michael tossed the cheap blade on the table. "Yeah."

"Not that." She pointed at Joto. "*That*."

Joto's eyes burned, red embers seared into white-hot flames. The fire spread as Samedi's face expanded across Joto's, covering the skin beneath with a gaunt, bony skull. Joto stayed where he was as another figure rose from him. Shadows flickered and took shape, and a series of hard angles became the Baron Samedi.

Danni dropped off the edge of the table and backed

away from him. The Baron advanced quickly, clamped a hand around her throat, and hefted her into the wall. She let loose a scream.

"I'm not impressed, *cher*. Not one bit."

Instinctively, Michael moved to intervene.

"Wait!" Joto shouted as he pivoted his chair across Michael's path. "That's her fight, Mike."

"He was going to let her die tonight!" Michael protested. "All for his twisted game!"

"Maybe," Joto said softly. "But it's *his* game."

Danni spoke through gritted teeth. "We found your stupid box."

"And lost your only means of opening it in the process!"

The Baron let her fall to her knees, but just as she began to catch her breath, his fingers wrenched her face back so his lips were inches from her ear.

"Make this right, Danielle. *Go home*."

He tossed her away again and flashed away in a pile of raining ash. Danni tried to stand but slumped back against the wall instead.

Michael shot a panicked look at Joto, who lifted his head, as if listening to something only he could hear. Finally, he eased his chair out of Michael's path.

"He's gone."

Michael sank to the floor and pulled Danni against his shoulder. Her head lolled against his hand. The normally bright blue centers of her eyes were glassed with pain. He reached for her pulse but stopped. The head of the nail glowed beneath her skin.

Michael searched Joto's face for answers but only found stone.

"I warned you," Joto said.

"Lecture me later!" Michael snapped. "Can you do something for her?"

Joto blew a heavy breath out his nose and pushed himself up to the table. He dumped a few dry herbs into the crucible and chased them with a clear fluid. The mixture steamed a cloud of yellowish fog into his face. He poured it out into a pewter cup and passed it to Michael.

"He's punishing her, Michael. Be safer for you to stay out of it."

Still, Michael coaxed the first sip into her mouth but lost most of it down her chin. He smoothed the hair back from her face and tried again.

"Come on, please. Just a little bit."

He tilted the pewter dish against her lips again. Her throat flexed, and she sputtered a cough.

A prayer fell out of his mouth quickly and quietly. "Remember most gracious Virgin Mary, that never was it known that anyone who fled to thy protection, implored thy help or sought thy intercession, was left unaided."

When he reached the end, he started again. "Remember most gracious Virgin Mary…"

Long seconds turned into longer minutes. Michael eyes flitted between her face and the glowing point in the center of her breastbone. Each time it started to fade, it would reignite.

"Remember most gracious Virgin Mary…"

Michael heard his voice break around the words, felt the tightness in throat, and the grief welling up behind that. It was too much to witness knowing he played a role in what she suffered now. Too much pain. Michael laid his cheek against hers and whispered into her ear.

"Come back to me, Danni. Please."

Her eyes shot open. She filled her lungs with wet and

desperate gasps. The ember in her chest faded. Michael cupped her face, searching her eyes as they began to clear.

"There you are," he whispered.

Danni nodded softly and flattened her hand against his.

"I'm okay," she whispered. She coughed again, and her voice found more weight. "I'm okay."

Michael held her face and checked her pulse.

Danni licked her lips and spoke around slow breaths. "Joto, can we use …the coin…to find…the koulev?"

Joto frowned. "Girl, please. You're bleedin' all over my damn floor."

Twenty-Eight

Four sisters stood in a semicircle in the hallway, their eyes downcast to the pale linoleum. Whatever prayer they spoke was too soft to be heard. When Michael reached the top of the stairs, Mary Claire saw him first and bit a rosy bottom lip between her teeth.

"She won't let us in."

Sister Charlotte followed his eyes to Danni's door.

"We could sit on her," she suggested grimly.

Sister Lavine shook her head. A veteran *Médecin Sans Frontiéres*, Michael trusted her opinion above all, and whatever brief assessment she'd been able to make had turned down the corners of her normally cheerful mouth. "She has at least three broken ribs. Maybe more."

"Would serve her right." Sister Bea breathed a small huff. "The *mouth* on that girl."

Michael swallowed a grin. "Let me see what I can do."

Sister Lavine started to object, but Michael only shook his head. "I won't hesitate to call you, I promise."

Danni heard the door creep off the threshold for a third time. The sound sent pulses of agony across every nerve ending. The shower had been torture enough, cleansing her of all the muck and blood until her skin burned bright pink. Though she was thankful for the loose sweats and a Mt. Carmel athletic department t-shirt they'd given her, what she needed now was a stiff drink and a fist full of pain killers. The sisters, however, were only offering fresh bandages and mentholated salve.

She kept her arm across her eyes as she spoke. "I said I was fine. Go pray or something."

"Heavenly Father, as it is here on Earth, so let it be from Heaven. I pray, Dear Lord, go ahead. Spit on her."

At the sound of his voice, Danni shot up on her elbows. Fresh pain ignited her ribs with an intensity that locked out her breath. She sank back against the feather pillow, lolling on her side as she tried to fill her lungs. Michael pressed the door back on the latch and stood there for a long moment.

She did her best to laugh, but it came out as a wheeze. "Where y'at?"

"What it is," he said softly.

"What it is, is painful."

He swallowed hard. "What can I do?"

Danni exhaled slowly. "Let me sleep?"

"You got it." Michael turned for the door.

"No," she said quietly. "Stay."

He kept his back to her for a long moment.

Danni continued. "The last time I slept safe was here with you. Maybe it was you. Maybe it was here. Right now..." She licked her dry lips. "I need both."

Michael wiped a hand across his mouth and turned to face her again. He moved to the bed but waited for her to adjust before stretching out beside her. She shifted down against the headboard and rested her head on his chest. The bed adjusted in a series of low creaks. Michael smoothed down the damp ends of her hair then wrapped a loose arm around her waist.

She hissed. "Ribs."

He slid his hand to her back and made slow circles with his thumb.

"I'm sorry," she said. "About the sisters. I'm…"

She let the words die. Like so many platitudes offered to those in mourning, they sounded hollow, empty in their own right, but it was the lie therein that hitched her voice.

"Not your fault," he said and then added. "Not mine either. As much as I want to believe I could have done more to protect them, I can't mourn them honestly if I'm still beating myself up over what I did or didn't do."

"Are we talking about the sisters or your brother?"

Michael sniffed a laugh. "Both, I think. He's never very far from me, always sitting on my shoulder, bugging me to do better. I thought he was annoying as a little brother, but as a guardian angel, he's relentless."

Danni smiled against his chest as her fingers traced an idle pattern against the smooth plane of his stomach. She let her mind wander in time with her hand, running over all the things she knew of the dead then realizing, she knew a lot less about the living.

"You ever think about leaving New Orleans?" she asked.

"Sure. I used to do it a lot. Still do sometimes." He closed his eyes and pulled in a long breath. "I'm driving out of town, headed east, racing against the oncoming darkness. I drive all day and then, like magic, I'm there."

"There?"

"Cape Canaveral. The next morning, I catch a rocket ship into space." Michael let out a long sigh.

"Astronaut Michael?"

"Oh yeah, had the cereal box layout all designed in my head." He turned his face into the top of her head. "But childhood dreams in the Lower Ninth are like the lottery, always in your head, never in your hands. They get you by while you work the days. Then you find new ones. Hopefully ones that, with enough desire and care and feeding, you can make real.

"How about you, you ever think about leaving?" he asked.

The answer came unbidden, out before she could think to call it back. "Every day."

Despite being an innocent confession, Danni's voice broke around it, breath hitched in to hide a sob. What little relief she found next to him vanished under a limitless amount of guilt. Every muscle constricted to shut out the truths she held so perilously in check.

She imagined herself like New Orleans, overrun by a perfect storm of the past, the present, and the uncertain future. For a few breathless moments, she let the tide take her. Let it grind down the thin resistance her body formed against it as his gentle hand rubbed rhythmic circles against her back.

"If it means anything to you," he said quietly, "I'm glad you didn't."

Twenty-Nine

Michael awoke to the afternoon sun in his eyes and the sound of a shower running. He slipped out the door and headed for the kitchen. A few minutes later he was back, knocking softly.

"If you don't have coffee, you don't have a chance of surviving the next knock," Danni called through the door.

He cracked it open far enough to extend a coffee cup through the gap. Her soft fingers withdrew it from him, and a second later, she opened the door.

"Okay, you get a reprieve."

Michael held up an orange and a pear.

"And admittance."

She reached for the pear and took a bite before moving deeper into the room. He pushed the door closed behind him, but kept his eyes on her. Overnight, her strength seemed to have returned and her steps were no longer stilted with pain. In fact, she seemed to be full of energy.

She eyed him over the edge of the coffee. "We slept late."

"You needed it."

"And you didn't?" She chucked a thumb at the bed. "When I climbed over you, your snoring didn't even slow down."

"I'll have you know I have *never* heard myself snore."

"Then you're deaf, too." She took another bite of the pear. "This place has the most wonderful fruit."

"Some of it's grown in the courtyard, the rest shows up from the Farmer's Market each morning."

"Nice to have some pull, hey?"

Michael smiled. "I used to have the job of unloading the morning deliveries. A farmer once told me, 'We say thank you when the sun shines for all that the sisters do for us when it doesn't.' When I think of it now, it reminds me of the commitments we share with the people here, the obligations to them."

Danni finished the pear and tossed the core in the trash.

"Orange?" he answered.

"You want half?"

He nodded, dug a thumb into the rind, and popped a slice into his mouth. It squirted against his teeth, sweet and wet and cool going down his throat.

"This is wonderful. You've got to have some."

He pulled a wedge free and reached for her just as she stepped forward. It hit her face and slid across her cheek before she caught his wrist.

"Oh, I'm sor—"

Her cheek. It had been so damaged, so painful to look at. Now, it was smooth and flawless and *perfect*. Michael was so distracted, he almost didn't notice her pull his hand to her lips to take the orange slice from it. The feel of her lips against his fingers was electric, mesmerizing. When he pulled his hand back, she came with it.

"I ... I don't want any more orange," he said and bent

187

his head to hers.

Her lips tasted like fruit, and fire, and…

Heaven.

The longer it lasted, the deeper they went. It left him dimly aware of a truth he only suspected before.

I could drown in this woman.

Michael rocked his forehead against hers. His breath caught with every quick lungful of air.

"Danni, *wait*."

She went lax against him but didn't move away. Her dark lashes swept down to rest against her white cheekbones, her gaze locked on his mouth.

"I can admit I want you, Michael. Tell me you don't feel the same thing."

She closed her mouth around his again. The fresh scent of oranges co-mingled with coffee flooded over his senses as her tongue slipped past his lips. Her nails raked a path up the taut skin beneath his shirt. She led him backward with the pressure of her mouth against his and used her body to hold him against the wall.

Danni strained into his touch, tentative at first, and then more eager. Her shirt was over her head with a swift jerk that broke her mouth from his before it came down again in a ravenous trail of kisses against his collarbone. She drew his hand back to her breast and moaned into his mouth.

Heat poured across Danni's chest. Her lips traced the line of his shoulder up to the pulse slamming in his neck. It pounded against her tongue, thick, rich, and real. It rose to meet her, white and soft, overwhelming in the moment but not unpleasantly so. She tested the sensation. It moved without hesitation, jumping from him to her in a flurry of images.

What started as a violent, white storm began to shift into dusky faces. Some she knew, others she did not. She recognized a much younger Sister Ned, at a time when her white tease of hair was more coffee than cream and the creases in her smile weren't quite as deep. Her eyes were the same warm hazel. They were looking *down* at her, at Michael.

Sister Ned lifted him easily and turned a quick circle. Danni felt the air against his face and his feet swung out behind him. The vision blurred from Sister Ned's face, but the sensation of spinning did not. She heard the melodic hoot of a pipe organ and smelled the sugar and cinnamon in the air. This time, a child smiled up at Michael from back of a stately unicorn. Together, they whirled around a glistening landscape of paper streamers and free-floating balloons. Bluesland.

Each slam of his pulse flooded another fresh rush down Danni's throat until extracting herself became impossible. Michael's hands held her in place, eliciting fresh waves of bliss as his fingers moved against her skin. She melted into him, letting the momentum carry her deeper into his history.

When memories of fast rides and open air faded, new images rose in their place, all connected on a central theme. When he wasn't spinning, he was driving at breakneck speeds through the wet air of a Louisiana summer. What had delighted him about the Mercedes made perfect sense.

Michael had always wanted to fly.

Danni knew it was everything he felt now with his lips locked to hers. His hands coasted the lines of her back, pulling her into him, rising with her. Free-falling off a precipice and reaching a weightless, terminal velocity as the true mysteries of his soul unwound against her.

No, not her. *The nail.*

Her mind seized around the sudden awareness. His soul was being sucked, quite literally, out of him. Her mind begged her to stop, but her body would not comply, ordered by the same magic that bound her with the Baron.

Panicked, Danni's eyes opened, but Michael was lost in the kiss. Could he sense it?

"Do they ever, *cher*?" the Baron chuckled.

In the space behind her eyes, Danni saw Samedi hued in purple light. He drifted through her conscious mind, prowling and hungry, as the first white threads of Michael's soul met the Crossroads. Power ignited, like two twisted points of lightning meeting over a plain. Michael's soul wound itself around the Crossroads, drawn into it through her.

It shouldn't have been possible. Not this way, not without the knife. But the how and the why weren't nearly as important as stopping it. Danni moaned into his mouth. What she'd meant as distress, he read as desire. He moved deeper into her mouth. The Baron laughed, and the sound dug in like a razor across her spine.

Suddenly the air shifted behind her, and a newly opened space was filled with a single, soft gasp. Michael tore his mouth from Danni's, and they both startled around to see Sister Mary Claire.

A blush spread pink across her nose as her eyes dove to the floor. "Excuse me."

Thankful disbelief flooded out of Danni as Mary Claire pulled the door closed behind her. The shock of intrusion was enough to break her pull on Michael's soul.

Michael staggered toward the bed, caught himself, and then leaned into the wall. She reached for him.

"Michael, are you…"

The shock in her eyes became the burn of unshed tears as she saw the confusion and fear in his. He shoved himself away from the wall, on a direct path for the door, but kept a hand held out to stop her from advancing any closer.

"I have to go."

Thirty

Michael closed the door quietly behind him. He didn't look at any of the sisters, but he could feel their eyes on him as he passed through the common room. He went to the kitchen, opened the freezer, and grabbed an ice cube from a tray. He stood over the sink and held it pressed between his wrists.

"That only works for heat from the outside," a stern voice said behind him. *Sister Ned.*

"That didn't take long," Michael said. "Mother Superior?"

"She's probably hearing about it now."

"Gossip flies on angel's wings."

"Don't be too hard on Mary Claire. It's not often she gets to be the bearer of something new." Ned's reflection grinned at him in the backsplash of the sink. "Let alone something salacious."

Michael turned to face her, and the smile faded from her eyes. "More important is what your intentions are. Mother Superior will expect you to know."

He sighed and pushed a hand through his hair. "I'm afraid I may fall short this time. I'm so out of control on this."

Sister Ned frowned. "Pride is still a sin, young man. Control rests in hands less earthly than ours."

"It wasn't temptation," he said. "I think I love her."

"You think? Or you know?"

There was a difference. He knew that much, and he nodded his understanding.

"I know I do."

"How does Danni feel?"

Michael shook his head, as much in response to clear the lingering fuzz from his brain. "That I don't know."

"You'd best be finding out then." Sister Ned held up a single, knotted finger. "But first, you go talk to Mother. Let her get a handle on the rumor mill before it spins into a soap opera. She's got enough on her plate."

"Enough on her plate? What do you – wait, what are you doing here, anyway?"

"She's pulled us all in. Even Sister Patrice."

"And her cats?"

"All twelve of them. Dropped off by a hotel van. Gabriel and I came over on the back of one of those bicycle rickshaw contraptions. Some nice, athletic young man peddled us all the way here. He had strong muscular thighs and a very firm backside."

"Why, Sister Ned."

"Yeah, look who's talking," she answered. "Mother said she wanted us close after something that happened last night. Don't suppose you know anything about that?"

"I might," he said.

He told her about Club Lakou, the koulev, and finally the missing sisters. They shared a long moment of silence before Sister Ned looked at him again, but the grief weighted her voice.

"I can see why she wanted us here, then. All the more reason for you to go talk to her, help her put it out of her mind. Tell her what happened, as much as is appropriate, of course. And then tell her you're going to pray on it."

Michael nodded once and started for the door. Sister Ned's voice stopped him.

"And, Michael?" He turned to her. "When you're done? Make sure you do it," she said.

He headed back to his room. It was only a little larger than the rest of the dormitories but sat off the western-most wing of the chapel. It seemed oddly vacant for a place he'd spent most of his adult life, except for the few trinkets he'd collected over the years. A felt Saint's pennant flag, a flattened penny from the railroad tracks where he'd grown up, and a photo of him, his mother, and Joey the one and only time he could recall them being together at the Mardi Gras parade.

He noted that his bed had already been changed for the day and fresh towels set out beside the sink. Shame came from knowing whoever had been tasked with morning linens definitely knew he hadn't slept there. He stared at the single kneeler against the far wall and felt a new twinge of guilt.

He would tell her today. He had to, but first …

He picked up the portmanteau from the short table beside the bed and made his way toward Mother Superior's office. Halfway there, the stairway began to shake. Noise echoed off the ceiling and walls.

Michael changed course for the common room, jogging and then running as the alarms began to sound.

Thirty-One

Danni paced the length of the room, swallowing big, settling breaths. Her hand ran over the nail buried in her breastbone and the sliver of heat in the metal: Michael's soul or at least part of it.

"Where are you?" she growled to the empty room. "Show yourself!"

If the Baron heard her, his answer was silence. Danni's fist met the wall. The skin peeled back from her knuckles and left a faint red imprint in the stucco. Fresh pain beat back the rise of tears as she flexed her hand and worked the blood to the surface.

"You fucking coward!"

A rumble passed through the floor. Danni moved to the window to search the street. They'd left the Mercedes just outside the delivery door next to a Dumpster. Heat waves baked off the cluster of black bags as seagulls dove and pecked at each other for scraps.

Another rumble passed deeper beneath the building. The short silence that followed was filled by screaming fire alarms. Danni threw open the door and started down the stairs, breaking into a full run when she heard the sisters' voices echoing from farther down the hall.

The sisters raced this way and that through the common room. What might have been a panicked charge for any other group was an orderly sprint for them, soundless except the shuffle of their shoes and the occasional outburst of commands.

The crowd parted for a second, and Danni saw the gaping hole in the center of the floor. Loose tile hung over the edge, pulling tables and chairs toward the slanted void. Mist and stink roiled up to her nose. The koulev.

She searched the room for Michael and found him on the other end, rushing a loose line of sisters through the exterior door. Those who stayed opened steel closets to fully-stocked armories. Sister Charlotte angled the barrel of a rifle over the top of a heavy oak buffet that had been toppled onto its side, while others battened the doors that led deeper into the building.

Danni was in search of a weapon bigger than a butter knife when a shotgun was thrust into her arms.

"Believe you're looking for that, dear heart." Sister Ned gave her an appraising look and rested a camouflaged .12 gauge against her own shoulder.

Danni racked a round, gave the sister a swift nod, and started to head for higher ground when a chilly little hand caught her elbow.

"Saint Michael the Archangel, defend her in battle. Be her protection against the wickedness and snares of the Devil. Amen." Sister Ned patted Danni's arm. "Okay, now go."

The common room was much smaller than the arena at Club Lakou with only a little more cover. Twelve low beams held the walk-around balcony in balance, while two iron chandeliers provided all the light. Danni jumped to the top of a long table and began calling off orders to the battalion of sisters.

"Get as much cover as you can!"

She was vaguely aware of Michael as he moved toward Sister Ned, as well as the hushed exchange of words that were no doubt his final attempt at convincing her to leave. Sister Ned proved her resolve by kneeling behind a table and balancing the barrel of the shotgun over the top.

The fire alarms died, but the dull screech continued in Danni's ears for several seconds to follow.

Roben clucked his tongue from the balcony above her. His neck craned out from the collar of a banana yellow suit, the *vire-pyes* in one hand and in the other ...

"Gabriel!" Danni screamed.

Roben held him easily, one hand gripping the back of his shirt as Gabriel kicked his feet over the floor.

"We can end this now," Roben said. "Before anyone gets hurt."

The other half of the coin was heavy in Danni's pocket. "You're right. We can."

Roben flashed a smile that quickly melted to a sneer. "You really think you can protect this boy, *all* these sisters, maybe get this coin, *and* kill what's coming out that hole? You're good. But you ain't that good."

He was right. One thing would come at the cost of another even with Michael's help. She watched Michael work his way around the edge of the room, a pistol resting awkwardly in his grip. She flicked her eyes from his face to Roben's and back again.

Michael shook his head.

Another rumble shook the floor. It rattled a chair over the edge and into the abyss. It reappeared a split second later, carried in on the head of the koulev. Open jaws snapped the chair into pieces as its head rose toward the ceiling.

Danni didn't wait for it to find her. She fixed sights on its head and squeezed the trigger. The sound echoed back loud and hard under the vaulted ceiling. The koulev screamed. Fresh blood fell across the tables. It slung its head side to side. Danni realized its yellow eyes were glassed over. *Blind.*

She jumped to the floor, sailed over the trench, and brought up the gun again. Bullets bit chunks from its side but also seemed to give it a sense of direction. It reared back and struck at her. Danni rolled beneath a table. It struck again before she could recover. The tabletop split. Through the crack she could see it winding back for another strike. Danni kicked herself backward just before it shattered through the wood and into the floor.

The koulev circled madly, hunting for her. It threw another blind strike against a support pillar hiding a cluster of nuns. Danni heard a gasp and recognized the blushing, narrow face of Mary Claire. Unfortunately, so did the koulev. It zeroed in on the sound and cranked back for a second strike.

"Hey! Over here!" Michael yelled.

He fired the gun into the floor in front of him, and the snake spun to face him.

Danni sprinted away from the wall, advancing on the back end of the snake as it moved toward Michael. She fired her last shell into the back of its head, knocking it forward.

The shotgun fell away. She bounded over the snake's body and latched on to the back if its head. Her heels dug into its side. Keeping its attention off the sisters and

Michael wouldn't be difficult until she grew tired or it smacked her into a wall.

It whipped her forward and back, trying to shake her, then to scrape her off. She let go just in time for its head to connect with the kitchen-side wall. She raced toward the opposite wall, screaming for its attention, but also for Michael's.

"Roben! Shoot Roben!"

She lost sight of him when the koulev struck again. Its bottom jaw connected with her shoulder and spun her into the wall. Pain arced through her back and knocked the wind out of her.

When it struck again, Danni planted her knees into its chest and fought it back from her face. The rank smell of blood rolled from its throat. It gnashed its fangs and hissed. A white glint caught Danni's eye. Her knife was still wedged in the back of its mouth.

Michael finally found his shot and fired into the wall beside Roben. The sound caused Roben to lose his grip on Gabriel. The boy tumbled toward the floor. Michael dove for him but caught empty air when Gabriel disappeared in a streak of yellow.

He flashed across the koulev's tail. It roared and rose up. Its jaws unhinged and the snake's head lunged down at Gabriel.

The wall erupted and rained plaster. The shotgun in Sister Ned's hands was only slightly louder than her screams of rage. She marched forward, out and around the heavy oak table she'd been using as shelter. Her hands pumped shells so fast the shots and their echoes sounded, indeed, like thunder.

The koulev shrieked, huge hunks of flesh disappearing as Sister Ned's shots found their mark. It wheeled back, seeking shelter from the onslaught.

But it recovered quickly, chasing Sister Ned down in three quick rushes. Danni leapt to the table and toward the chandelier. She used her momentum to swing wide, kicking her legs and slinging herself back to land between Sister Ned and the koulev.

Michael's gun sounded far away as he emptied the clip. The snake jerked back a few paces, leaving Danni enough time to relocate them all behind another pillar. She held a long finger to where Roben watched overhead.

"Will you please shoot that son of a bitch and get me the other half of the coin?" she screamed at Michael.

Still, Michael hesitated

"He won't do that," Roben called.

He jumped from the balcony in one long leap, and landed behind Michael. "Priests don't kill."

Danni's eyes locked with Michael's. Her breath shuddered out in small pants.

"Priest," she repeated.

She searched his face and then looked at Sister Ned, finding nothing but sorrow. She turned back to Michael.

"You're a priest?"

He didn't answer. He didn't need to. The pieces slid together like a frantic mosaic, culminating around one central moment when his lips met hers.

He didn't love her. He couldn't. He'd been seduced by her and *that* had been the Baron's game the entire time.

Shocked, Danni staggered backwards. The koulev struck the center of the pole at her back. It sent a cloud of plaster dust between them. Danni turned her face toward the ceiling, her mind to the Crossroads, and screamed.

"*Akeyi yo, Baron!*"

The koulev froze, its head reared back and jaws open. A small cloud of red smoke appeared in front of Danni. It rolled and grew and then, just as quickly, it faded from the inside out. Samedi stood in its place.

"You rang, *cher*?"

"I need to use my boon."

"Of course." He laced his fingers together and cracked his knuckles. "Shall I tie this creature into a knot for you? How about a puppy dog or a flower?"

As pleasing a suggestion as it was, Danni shook her head. "I want the other half of the vire-pyes."

"Ah. Very well, *cher.*"

The Baron snapped once and unfolded his gloved hand. The coin sat on the tip of his index finger. She snatched it without hesitation.

"You take all the fun out of moments like these, you know?" he grumbled. Then he vanished.

She ripped the other coin from her pocket. The two halves came together in her fist, ignited by the magic that bound them face-to-face. It began to hum with incandescent energy, warming her palm and spilling across her chest.

The koulev struck the pillar again, crushing the support but miring itself in the metal mesh housed in the center of the poured cement.

Danni brandished the coin. The koulev snarled and hissed, shaking off the tangle of metal before fixing a white eye on her hand.

"That's right," she whispered. "Watch the coin."

The koulev cooed and settled, bringing its head down to

Danni as she took a tentative step forward. She heard a rattling whisper in her ear that was surprisingly feminine.

Missssstressss

"There you go." Danni waved it in closer until she could extend her arm to touch the koulev's bloodied face.

Hunnngrey.

"Open your mouth," Danni said.

It did. The knife sat buried to the hilt in the back of its throat. Danni extended a slow hand between the glistening rows of teeth.

"If you bite me, I swear, you'll be shoes tomorrow."

The koulev made a painful sound as Danni jerked the knife free. It sagged and laid its blood-soaked face against Danni's shoulder.

Hhhhurt.

Danni couldn't help but feel empathy for the thing. A dog was only as good as its master. She glanced back at Roben's startled face and then looked at the koulev again.

"Listen to me," Danni said softly. "No more nuns. Or children. Or people in general. I let you go, you head for the lake. More than enough fish and gators to keep you happy."

The koulev nodded. *Yesss, Missssstresss.*

"Go on, now. Get out of here."

Danni watched it back away, more consumed with its wealth of injuries than with anyone else in the room. Still, she followed it with the coin in one hand and the knife in the other. The koulev sank into the hole and out of sight.

Michael turned and swung his fist into Roben's face. Roben staggered back, cupping a hand to his nose as it gushed blood down the bright yellow suit. Michael started toward him again, but Sister Ned held him back.

"This isn't our way," she said.

Roben kept a careful eye on them as he backed toward the nearest door. He stumbled over his own feet, frantically searching each of their faces. Sister Ned's and Michael's. Then Danni's.

His voice sounded wet beneath his hand. "He'll kill me!"

Danni didn't bother to ask who. She didn't care. She palmed the knife and turned the blade around in her fist. "So will I."

He scrambled and fell into the door. She watched him stumble down the street as it swung back to the threshold. The lock snapped hard, leaving no sound except the dull whine in her ears.

The sisters rose from their hiding places. Danni walked slowly around the room, kicking over the shattered remains of the tables and chairs. The portmanteau sat on the only unbroken piece of furniture, a white-oak pillar.

Danni ran her hand over the smooth skin and found the depression in the top. Michael took a single step toward her but stopped.

A priest.

Danni wrenched her fist around the knife and slammed it into the top of the box.

Thirty-Two

White light split her vision as the warm flare opened across her face. The shimmering stream of souls rose around her. They called her name, a sweet and melodious hymn of voices. It swelled into a full chorus before fading off into some unseen distance followed by silence. The sheen of the portmanteau died.

The Baron Samedi swung his feet over the balcony edge.

"Well done, *cher. Well done.*"

He jumped as he reached the hole in the floor, evaporating into a cloud that spread and came together again on the other side. His simple tuxedo was replaced with an ivory, double-breasted jacket trimmed in gold. Ten buttons held it together at his waist before it flared out to the matching knee breeches. Party clothes.

He swept Danni against him, one hand on her waist and the other against her neck. He dipped her toward the floor and blew a hot breath over her lips. Blood, the koulev's and her own, melted off her face as a tingle passed up her spine. When he released her again, she was clean of any indication of the battle she'd just fought and won. Or fought and lost. She couldn't decide.

The Baron bowed. "Come, *cher*. We'll celebrate."

"I don't think so, brother!"

The Baron LaCroix stood across the pit bathed in a red glow of mist. "It was my man who found the portmanteau. The celebration is ours."

Samedi tipped his head back and laughed. "*Au contraire*, brother. He may have laid first hands on it, but she freed the souls."

"She would never have had the opportunity to release the souls were it not for your interference!"

Smugly, Samedi spread his hands wide and shrugged. "I did only what I was obligated to do."

"And your obligation to this *fème* outweighs your obligation to me?" LaCroix seethed. "I demand *parle*!"

The room slowed to a crawl and then went still. Dust hung in the air around the sisters who also seemed to be frozen in place. Samedi whipped his hand around a small cluster of broken chairs. The pieces began to reorder themselves to whole. He waited for his brother to sit then gestured for Danni and Michael to do the same.

Michael did but Danni remained motionless. Samedi's finger drew an invisible circle in the air beside his head.

"*Sit*," he said.

Something wrenched in the center of her chest and she collapsed into the chair.

The Baron Cemetrie appeared in a column of white and blue smoke. He was dressed with a series of archaic runes stitched into his loose fitting linen shirt. The only sprig of color came from a small blue feather stuck into his white hat band.

"Let *parlé* begin!" He tipped the hat back on his head

and sucked at the edge of his tooth. "What now?"

"The blade was in *cher's* hands when the souls were released," Samedi said.

"Only due to your interference," LaCroix replied.

"It may very well have happened without my granting her the boon which, I remind you both, I was obligated by prior agreements to grant. Besides ... " Samedi sniffed a laugh. "Your boy *could* have seized control of the coins and the snake, were he willing to put a bullet in the right spot."

LaCroix's eyes burned. "You. Cheated."

"You both cheated," Danni interrupted.

She pointed a finger at Samedi. "*You* sent Gabriel and the other children to paint the toby at Bluesland then used Joto to convince Michael to find me."

Then she looked at LaCroix. "*You* left the card with Sister Ned that took us to Holy Cross."

Finally she faced Cemetrie. "They both were at Club Lakou, which, by the way, *thank you* for letting that snake almost kill me."

LaCroix looked angry. Samedi made a show of being bored, and patted a gloved hand over an open-mouthed yawn.

"*Cher*, the snake never stood a chance. Besides, *I* didn't burn down your apartment."

All eyes shifted to LaCroix, who offered a sheepish grin.

"Why would you even do that?" Michael asked LaCroix.

LaCroix scoffed. "Well, *your* bed didn't seem to interest her at the time."

Michael winced. Danni continued. "More like, you needed us together for your twisted game to continue. You've both been playing with us from the beginning, but that's all this has ever been about! Your stupid fucking game!"

Samedi snapped and Danni doubled over her knees. "Manners, *cher*."

Michael reached for her. She shoved his hand away.

If Cemetrie observed any of it, he gave no sign. "Clearly, the boon was owed," he said finally.

Samedi grinned, triumphant.

Cemetrie continued. "Just as clearly, it changed the outcome of the events, and the balance of the game. In this case, for the girl. So, let the opportunity exist for the boy as well. LaCroix, you may grant him a boon as well."

Samedi stood to protest but Cemetrie held up a hand. "It can be for nothing more substantial than what was given to the girl. If he is as clever as she? The scales are balanced. If he is more so, he would have won, anyway."

Neither Samedi nor LaCroix looked particularly pleased, but they remained silent.

"So." Cemetrie settled his hat back on his head and touched his hat brim with two fingers. "Let the game continue."

He stood but paused, nodding slightly at where Danni sat hunched over her knees and clutching her chest.

"Mercy, brother. You got what you wanted," he said. He vanished from the sandals up.

Samedi made a dismissive gesture and spit at the floor in his wake. The pain in Danni's chest released and she sat back in the chair, panting. Michael reached for her again, but this time her voice was full of a heat.

"Don't touch me."

LaCroix stood and tapped a finger against the top of Michael's head.

"So, it seems you have a boon." A mist rose around his

feet and he disappeared within it, but his voice echoed after him. "Don't waste it."

Samedi rolled his eyes. "Always with the drama. Don't fret it, *cher*. He'll fuck that up, too."

And he, too, disappeared.

Danni's eyes shifted to the grandfather clock at the back of the room. The pendulum stayed still for a second longer then swung back into normal rhythm. Motion in the room resumed. Sister Mary Claire and Sister Charlotte reached for each other as Sister Ned stepped forward to touch Michael's shoulder. Two painfully green eyes searched Danni's face.

"Danni … " he started.

She turned to face him fully, wiping the blade against her hip. Her eyes fell to the portmanteau again and she lifted it from the table.

For an object of such great value, it was startlingly small. Light. *Empty.* She held Michael's eyes for a moment longer and then spiked it at his feet.

Michael watched as a thousand brittle pieces of the portmanteau skittered outward across the room. He looked up only just in time to see Danni disappear around the corner.

He started after her but Sister Ned held firm to his arm. "Not yet."

"Not yet?"

She sighed. "She's hurt and she's angry. She needs her own time, to find her own way. Same as you."

She pulled him aside as her voice became a whisper for his ears alone. "Michael. You never told her you were a priest."

"I was—"

"That wasn't a question, boy," she snapped.

Her tone softened again. "But I do have one for you. *Why?*"

Thirty-Three

"O my God, I am heartily sorry that I have offended you because I dread the loss of heaven, and fear the pains of hell … "

Michael's prayer faltered. When had the pains of hell become so abstract? Until that moment, they'd never felt quite as real.

He rolled a sore shoulder, and looked at the bruises on his knuckles. Physical wounds would heal much faster than the spiritual ones. His confession to Mother Superior had made that clear enough.

"Wounds of the flesh and wounds of the heart. Tend to both, lest they feed on each other instead." He knew it made sense, at least to her. "But words without deeds do nothing."

He caught a twisted reflection of his face in the smoked glass that lined the walls near the altar. He wanted to act. Instead, she had sent him here to meditate, pray. Settle his spirit.

But every time he closed his eyes, all he could see was Danni. The cold fire in her face, her rigid, angry stride as she left the convent. She had been everything the sisters had needed and more. He clasped his hands together, interlocked his fingers in front of him and closed his eyes.

"O my God, I am heartily sorry ... "

He began the liturgy and let the rhythm of the words carry him down and away. He opened his heart, admitted his feelings. The passion, the pain of loss, the shame of his indulgences. He pulled each thought out and held it up, trying to see it from every light.

Michael's mind floated. He let the words express the thoughts as they appeared, let his subconscious release the emotions behind each one.

Slowly, Danni came back, floating in front of him, the definition of his want. Not just a physical yearning but a complete one. He released a slow breath and let the vision of her solidify in his mind.

"Don't sweat it, *homme*. She does this to everyone."

The image began to change as Samedi stretched through her face. She turned to smoke and vanished behind him.

"She'd probably even do it to me, were I a man."

He tipped his hat forward and bounced back a few steps to the altar. His jacket matched the cream top hat on his head, white all the way to the riding boots that spanned knee to toe and were fastened with a long line of bone buttons. He cocked one foot against the top of the altar and let the other swing over the side.

"How are you here?" Michael demanded. "How can you be in this place?"

The Baron held his arms wide, a mock pose of the crucifix above him.

"I'm not in this place. I'm in *you*."

"That's impossible."

"Is it?" Samedi sat up, dropped his feet to the floor and let Michael considered him fully. "Haven't felt right since she left, have ya? Haven't felt quite whole."

"I—" Michael stopped, cleared his throat, and tried again. "I love her. And now I feel like a part of me is gone."

Samedi chortled. "She took a piece of you. I'll give you that one for free."

"What are you talking about?"

Samedi pulled a fresh rumrunner from his pocket and held the tip to a prayer candle. He took an exaggerated drag and then blew the smoke out to thick cloud. His fingers whipped it into Danni's silhouette again.

"Have you ever been to the circus, Michael? They have all these animals. Elephants, bears, lions, all gentled down and sad. Except for the tigers."

The image shimmered and began to move, a soundless laugh caught in the half-open swell of her mouth. One slender, smoky arm reached for Michael's face, but he batted it away.

Samedi traced a bladed fingernail across the thin, hard line of her jaw.

"You can't beat that instinct out of them. Years of evolution have shaped and molded them until they have only one true purpose."

Again the smoke rose in her image, but this time the laughter became rage. Her face contorted into angry, vicious lines. She rushed at Michael and broke around him. He coughed against the sweetness in the smoke and waved it away from his face.

"Leave," he growled.

"Careful, boy."

Samedi dropped down from the altar and closed his fist in the air. A sudden, sharp pull in the middle of Michael's chest dragged him to the floor.

"Feel that?" Samedi snarled.

Michael tried for a smooth breath only to find it locked out under several hundred pounds of pressure. His instinct was to reach for his rosary, but his hand stopped short as Samedi demonstrated his new found control.

Still, Michael fought him and clenched his fist against his chest. Something burned in the back of his throat, and for a second he imagined it was the smoke from the rumrunner, but it was different. Thicker. Sickly sweet and rotten. When he lifted his eyes from the floor, he knew it was Samedi's breath.

"How?" Michael wheezed.

"It's what she was built to do. She carved out a piece of you and brought it back to her master."

Michael's mind flashed back through the days until they landed on one moment.

"*I* kissed her." It sounded desperate, even to him. He shook his head and tried again. "She wasn't trying to…"

"She did as I bid her." Samedi grinned, and Michael could see the stark image of the skull appearing through his skin.

"It is the mistake of every man, *homme*. Drinking poison because it tastes like wine. Get comfortable with it." Samedi patted his cheek. "Finish your prayers. We'll talk again soon."

Thirty-Four

Hammers and saws, the song of mourning and resurrection. In New Orleans, both started almost immediately after a disaster.

Or devastation.

Michael found a place to fill in and help. He hauled bracing lumber and fresh flooring. He hammered supports and plywood into place. It took a while, but his hands finally stopped shaking enough to hit nails more often than wood.

The violence inside the convent had not been quiet. Spectators appeared from around the neighborhood, first peering carefully around doors and then quickly becoming volunteers that came and went throughout the night. The sisters worked alongside them, ministering to each other and to their neighbors, calming each other as they calmed their community.

Michael kept to himself and kept working.

When the flooring was finished, he started on the walls, carefully prying and carving bullets from the woodwork. Then spackle and putty and patches. Around him, the night bled into morning and morning into afternoon. He was wearily negotiating the delivery of more supplies when a hand pulled the phone from him and closed it.

Sister Ned's look was as firm as her grip. "Someone else will call them back. Time for you to be still, boy."

Boy… not Father.

"I see the gossip train ran on time," he said.

"Official church business is not gossip," she answered. "Well, not always. Come with me."

She marched away, leaving him no choice but to follow. He was afraid for a moment that she was leading him back to the chapel but she passed the doorway without slowing down. Instead of leading him back to his room, she took him upstairs. To Danni's room, or what had been her room. Sister Ned pointed to a pair of chairs that had been placed near the narrow window. The bedside table had been moved between them, and a teapot and tray had been left atop it.

"Sit. Eat. Rest."

"I have a bed," he said stiffly.

Sister Ned didn't flinch. "Sister Levine is using your room to house a few of the more grievously wounded for the time being."

Michael felt the tension leave his throat only for guilt to replace it. "I didn't realize…"

Ned waved him off. "Cuts and bruises. Mary Claire broke her arm." She nodded toward the bed. "You can sleep here if you've a mind to."

"Thank you."

"You're quite welcome." She poured them tea and sat in the chair opposite him.

Michael stared at the walls. There was a wet section where something had been scrubbed from the stucco. He pressed his fingers into the dull stain and lifted it to his nose. He recognized the faint scent of blood.

"Drink your tea," Ned said. "You need something more inside you than grief."

Dutifully, he took the cup in both hands and held it to his lips. Notes of lavender and orange drifted across the top. The lavender made sense, but the orange?

No, the orange was already in the room. Even as he smelled it he remembered the taste of it on his tongue and the wetness against his lips. He dropped the cup on the table and felt the sharp burn as the liquid splashed over the rim.

"You ready to talk about it?" Sister Ned asked.

His head swam as he tried to piece together just which *it* she might mean.

She went on. "You were in the chapel for hours. You came out shaking and pale as a ghost. Not exactly the composure of one who has made his peace with the Lord."

He grimaced. Lord? Not by a long shot.

"You know," she said. "You never were much for confessions, taking or giving."

"What's that supposed to mean?" he said hotly.

"You make a good effort when it comes to acts and generosity, just not much in the confessional, is all."

Michael turned up his palms. "Too many people think it's a get out of jail free card. Say a handful of Hail Mary's and go do it again. It's not like I was kidding anybody."

"Still aren't," she said. "Except maybe yourself."

"It's not that simple."

"What is? Michael, let's be honest. You were never going to be a great priest. Not because you didn't know the words, you do. But you don't love the ceremony, the vespers and rituals and whatnot. It's not because you don't love the Lord, or care about the people. Heaven knows, you're filled with love for the church. You've got all that in spades. But you've got it for different reasons. Look at you. You aren't even comfortable in the clothes."

His head was swimming, under-currents and eddies pulling his thoughts in a dozen directions, and the tide was still coming in.

"Do you remember when you became an altar boy?" she asked.

"Sure. Some of the boys laughed, because I was so much older than them."

"They didn't laugh long, though, huh? You were dedicated, worked hard. Left them behind in a flash. Nobody could out-study you."

"Had to. I started late."

"Yes, you did. Why do you suppose that was?"

"Why I started late?"

"No. Why you became an altar boy."

"I just … I mean." The first answer that came to mind brought pain, shame, and blocked out any of the easy lies that might come to cover it.

"Come on. You can say it."

He sighed slowly. The breath ended in a word. "Joey."

"Joey," Sister Ned nodded. "I remember when you went off to seminary, your mother was so proud because you really were a good boy, and you weren't going to end up like … "

She let the thought die, but clearly only so he could finish it for her.

"That's cruel," he spit.

"Not cruel. Hard. The truth's a hard thing sometimes. So is love. You know your mother always loved you, boy. And she was proud of you."

"But part of it was always about Joey."

"Yes, it was. She was human. You know that. I bet you even forgave her for it."

"Of course I did."

Sister Ned watched him closely, tears shining in her eyes. "Of course you did. How about you? When are you going to forgive yourself?"

Michael felt his own tears coming to stand in the bottom of his eyes. He shook them away, still uncertain who he was even grieving for. His mother, his brother. The sisters. Danni. Himself?

"You were a good student," Sister Ned pressed. "What did Father Pat say about atonement?"

"That that job has somebody else's name on it," he said.

"And penance?"

"It's not a payback–"

"Just one of the paths to forgiving ourselves," they finished together.

"You see," she said. "Always the good student. Time to learn the lesson, boy. If you stay on one path forever, it's not a path anymore. It's a hiding place."

She stood in front of him and put her hands on his shoulders. "You're a good man, Michael. The Lord knows there's room in your heart for all kinds of love."

He looked up at her and covered the backs of her hands with his. "May not be room in hers for me, anymore."

"That's a new path. You'll just have to walk it and find out."

Thirty-Five

Go home.

She hadn't understood it at the time, but now it seemed
almost too simple as the late afternoon sun chased her over
the Twinspan. Lake Pontchartrain spilled out across the
horizon, sun-drenched, chopped water the color of polished
copper, radiant against the backdrop of lush, summery
green. Danni thumbed the stereo and cranked it up. A
smoke-throated woman's story of a deceitful lover carried
her across the channel.

The bridge ended on the westernmost edge of
Mandeville. The air this close to the lake was spiced with
cypress and juniper, far enough from the city to smell clean
and rich and white. New Orleans might as well have been a
world away. She passed sweeping cottonwoods and the
white-rocked driveways that led to large plantation homes
now fixed with modern conveniences. The city had sprung
for gas lanterns in the post-Katrina rebuild and they were
just kicking on as she reached Harper Street. She made a
full lap past the designer shops and their designer windows.

Her nails bit down hard on the steering wheel. In

retrospect, it had been obvious the day she met him: his careful avoidance, and his aloof explanations. She'd missed all the signs that pointed in the same direction. Then again, she wondered, how many had she missed, and how many had she willfully ignored?

She followed North Shore Drive past the marina where the houses were fewer and farther between. She pulled into a driveway, now more grass than gravel, and slowed as she reached the house.

Most of the side-gable had been lost in the storm leaving the upstairs open to the elements. Insulation puked from shattered plaster lath, baked yellow under the sun. Beneath the balcony frieze the row of French windows had been boarded with simple sheets of plywood.

The flower beds that had once been full of white caladiums and purple irises were now a thicket of mangrove and trumpet vines. She worked her way over a field of upturned landscaping stones half-buried in the dirt.

Danni jiggled the keys inside her fist and let her eyes wander out across the backyard. She'd once considered a pool or a dog. Anything to fill the empty rolling meadow that now held a shag of cinnamon straw grass well past her knees.

Her eyes swept across the property and stopped on an old well house. It was a little smaller than a single car garage with a shaker style roof, but she was certain it had never been there before. Like the mausoleum in Holy Cross cemetery had been, the well house looked like it had dropped out of the sky.

She moved toward it, keeping a hand against her chest. The nail flexed forth a feeling of profound grief and guilt.

The door was slatted wood and iron band but still solid. She jerked it off the threshold, unsurprised to find the third portmanteau seated in the cool dirt floor. Light bent around the top of the box as she held the door open with one foot to retrieve it.

She moved back toward the house. Curled paint crunched beneath her feet as she climbed the stairs and pushed the key into the lock. A grand staircase rose from the darkness of the foyer to an open balcony surrounded by a copse of snapped balusters. The floor groaned and popped, sagging in places as she secured her steps through the parlor and into the living room. Her arm swept hunks of ceiling plaster from the top of a built-in buffet. She set the portmanteau in the center.

She should have died here. She could still hear Hell unfolding around her as daylight shone through the slats of shuddering Wainscoting and the plaster coughed free from the walls. She stared at the east wall and the hole through what used to be her dining room. She hadn't given any of it much thought until today, when Michael's mouth had found hers, tentative at first and then harder and more real. She hadn't realized how much she wanted to reclaim everything she'd lost.

She wasn't sure how long she stood there rerunning the dim edges of a memory. But the sun was well behind the horizon and the buzz of nighttime creatures had crept its way into the house when the Baron appeared.

"I don't like seeing you like this, *cher.*"

Danni frowned and cast a long look over her shoulder. "*What do you want?*"

He shrugged, gave it some thought, and reached for her. "*You* not to look quite so *douloureux.*"

She pushed his hands away and wrapped her arms around her shoulders. "Not much left to be happy about, is there?"

The Baron circled around in front of her again, aghast. "All *this* because of Father What-A-Waste?"

"The truth," she said softly. "Is that why you want his soul? Because he's a priest, and you can't have him any other way?"

He wagged a playful finger in her face. "The truth costs, *cher*."

She shrugged. "Indulge me."

It seemed to amuse him. Samedi tucked his cane into his armpit and pushed back his sleeves. The cane spun out again, and he cracked it against the floor. The sound echoed up the walls before crashing back. Fresh light bled down the walls, restoring the plaster and re-coloring the tattered wallpaper. It reached the floor and continued beneath her feet, out and around the room, re-knitting the drapes, the carpet, the furniture. Everything she had once designed made whole again. He stepped off the distance to the formal living room, beckoning her as he went, and then turned out his tails to sit in the center of a red couch.

"You have always had remarkable taste, *cher*." His fingers cruised over the carved wood and plush fabric. "You were the one who first tasted the power inside him, and you would have given him to me then. True?"

She felt the tears rising in the bottom of her eyes and fought them, but finally gave in to let them roll down her cheeks. Danni nodded.

"We have a saying at the Crossroads. What's better than one soul? Five souls. What's better than five souls?" He leaned in over his crossed knee. "The soul of a man who belongs to another God. He is, quite literally, one in *millions*."

Danni drew a shaky breath. "He was your insurance policy, in case you couldn't beat LaCroix."

Samedi nodded knowingly. "Like I said, remarkable taste."

"All this, just to beat your brother," she whispered.

He shrugged. "These things, *cher*. It's what I do. What *we* do."

Danni ran a hand over the portmanteau, found the slit in the top, but made no move to draw the knife.

"Well, what are you waiting for?" he pressed. "Open it."

She held the box between them. "I want to make a deal."

He stood and narrowed his eyes. "Or what, *cher*?"

"Or I'll go back to the convent and let *him* open this."

"Are you *sure* that's a good idea?"

She wasn't, but only because she wasn't sure how she could face Michael. But she'd do it, if it meant costing the Baron his win.

"I'm sure LaCroix wouldn't mind," she added.

The Baron nodded. "That might work, but you're forgetting one thing, *cher*. There is still one more box to find."

"Pretty sure I know how." She stepped into him. "Joto said you sent Michael after me, but I didn't know why. I already had the knife. But he is the compass. At least, he *was*."

Danni tapped her breastbone, watching the Baron's eyes move to the metal secreted in her skin. "The part I took, it's the part of him that makes him a priest. The part that comforts the weary and offers them rest. It's why I could sleep when I was next to him."

Rage flared across the Baron's eyes as the white skull replaced the softer lines of his face. Cinder and smoke rose around them, clotting out the edges of the room and filling them with the scent of seared skin. There was ice in his voice when he spoke again.

"It seems you have somewhat of an advantage, *cher*. What, then, would you like to do with it?"

"Give it back to him."

"What?"

"Give it back," she repeated. "I'll open this and your last box, but once I do, I want you to give him back the piece of his soul that I took."

The Baron held his eyes on the portmanteau for a long moment. She ran a single finger across his lapel and closed her fist around the tingle of a pain that followed.

"Certainly one little priest is worth less than the entire Delta."

Danni watched as his hand unfolded through the smoke. The deal was struck in a swift handshake, but before he let go, he smothered the back of her hand with his.

"Even when I do restore Michael his soul, you'll still belong to me."

The ash began to settle but the house was fading with it. The broken boards and waterlogged couches reappeared.

"*Akeyi yo*, Baron. I know."

Thirty-Six

Michael swung wide around a curve as fast as the battered, old truck would take him. The bluish light was already beginning to fade into the clouds, and a few wrong turns in the maze of million-dollar homes had cost him precious time. He downshifted and let the truck coast across another bottomed-out intersection. His headlights flashed over the sleek body of the Mercedes farther up the road.

He jerked the truck through the gears and slowed just outside the shadow of what clearly had been a lovely house. Danni waited at the door.

"How did you find me?" she asked.

He pointed to the lingering haze of souls working free of the clouds. "You okay?"

She shrugged. "A little dopey. Twice in one day ... "

Dopey wasn't the right word, but drunk might have been. She weaved toward the Mercedes and the laid flat across the hood.

"What is this place?" Michael asked.

"My house."

"Big place for one person. Was it just you?"

She nodded.

"But you never came back after the storm," he said. "Why?"

She pressed her cheek to the hood and stared at the gaping hole in the side of the house. "I never left. I was here when Katrina hit." She closed one eye, squinted the other, and held the knife out to the further edge of the house. "Right *there*, actually."

Michael followed her eyes to where the roof had collapsed into the second floor. He shuddered at the thought but waited for her to continue.

"The night of the last evacuation, the power was already out. I was upstairs when the storm hit. The noise... I heard the sirens for a while but then even those stopped, and all I could hear was the lake roaring and the trees being torn out of the ground. When the roof caved in, I didn't even notice him at first. But then, he stood and dusted the plaster off his coat.

"Samedi," Michael whispered.

Danni nodded. "He was the most horrible thing I'd ever seen. He looked dead, and for a minute, I thought I was, too."

She made a noise between a laugh and a sob. "He'd dropped these little blue marbles all over the place... I took one. That was it. I didn't even realize it was a soul at the time. The next thing I know, he's holding me against the wall and slamming something into my chest."

She closed her eyes. "I'd never felt pain like that, and the entire time he was laughing, babbling in some language I didn't understand. I might have passed out, but when I woke up, I was in my bed with the knife on my pillow and a nail in my chest."

Danni slid off the hood of the car then reached into the

seat of the Mercedes for a fresh cigarette. She cupped the lighter inside her fist until the end burned red-hot.

"Samedi came to see me, too," Michael said. "Pushed his way into my prayers. Showed me my new leash."

Danni laughed. It sounded sick. "There is nothing he loves more than a good gloat." She sobered. "I'm taking care of it."

"What more could you have to give him? He already has you. Do you sacrifice someone else in my place?"

"I wouldn't do that," she said sharply. "I'll get you back the piece I took, and it won't cost anyone else's life."

"Just yours," he said.

She shook her head. "It wasn't really mine to begin with."

"It was at some point." He gestured to the house. "I didn't get it, but I think I do now. He's manipulating you, but not because you owe him a debt. You're trying to earn your freedom, aren't you?"

Danni shoved herself away from the car and walked out of his slow, advancing reach.

"Tell me what he promised you," he demanded.

"Nothing," she shouted. "It's what I do. What *we* do!"

Unconvinced, Michael tried again. "Damn it, Danni! I gave you that piece of me! Now tell me *why*!"

She ran a hand through her hair and walked out to a distance where twilight washed the color from her eyes.

"It was just a kiss, Michael."

His voice traveled across the rustle of overgrown grass, soft but full of steel. "It was more than that, and you know it."

"You're right," she said finally. "It was."

Danni closed the distance between them and reached up to the back of his head, pulling him against her roughly.

She rested her free hand up against his chest. His hands drew her closer, her mouth hard against his.

His tongue sought the inside of her mouth. Something stabbed inside his chest, a piercing jolt followed by a sharp tug that opened the rush of a quick fall beneath them. His eyes snapped open.

A drier, gritty heat filled the air around them. Instead of the silvery taste of the cigarette on her breath, he smelled the stench of burning sulfur and skin. Before he could place the scent, he saw it. A wide wall, rising on all sides. Faces screamed from an open abyss. The longer he stared, the louder they became.

They shrieked, calling her name. Then his. The sound bit at the back of his eyes. More voices rose, washing over in waves, crashing against his mind and leaving penetrating silence in their wake.

As quickly as it happened, it was over. Michael saw the ground rush up beneath him, registered the fall before he felt the gravel bite his knees. He ran a quivering hand across his bottom lip.

"The Crossroads?" he whispered.

Danni nodded. There was iron in her eyes. "Come near me again, and you'll never make it back."

Thirty-Seven

"I haven't been drunk since I was sixteen," Michael said.

"You still haven't," Joto answered.

Joto had made a little game of tossing pennies from the top of the steps to an empty shot glass in the alley. Michael watched another flash forward over and then heard it bounce against the asphalt. Joto poured out another shot and took it.

Michael set his own glass against the railing. It immediately started sliding toward the bottom step. Michael's hand moved to catch it about the same time as it shattered beneath the stairs.

"Okay, maybe you're a little drunk," Joto said.

"A little stupid." Michael scrubbed his eyes with the butts of his hands. "I thought I was a priest. Then I thought I was in love. I thought … I thought I could be the hero, J. I was gonna save somebody, everybody."

"Not for lack of trying," Joto said and passed him another shot. "But nobody saves everybody, Mike. Not even God."

Somewhere farther down the alley, a door slammed. Voices sang a drunken harmony in Latin, or German, or late night gibberish. It echoed off walls and then faded down the street. Joto motioned at him with two fingers, and Michael tossed back the shot. It definitely went down smoother than the first couple, but it still burned.

"What is that shit?"

"Bayou firewine." Joto held up the bottle proudly and swirled it in the light of the street lamp. "Ain't much more than moonshine with a few cayennes thrown in for flavor, but it'll lay you out right. Here. Have 'nother."

Michael waved off the glass. "I'm trying to forget her, not burn out my frontal lobe."

Joto shoved it at him again. "Might have to do just that to get her out of your brain. I ain't gonna lie to you, Mikey. She was—"

"Lie to me," Michael said quickly.

He jerked the glass from Joto's fingers. Most of it slopped over on his hand, but he swallowed the remainder and slammed the glass down on the step. "*Uhg*! That's still awful."

Joto sniffed the mouth of the bottle, shrugged, and took a long swig.

"So, what else you wanna do tonight, Not a Father Michael? Wanna get in a bar fight, maybe pick up a few ladies down in Treme?"

"Now you're just being a jerk."

"Nah, just wanna know how serious you are about this."

Michael wrung his hands together over the stairs and stared blankly into the spaces between the slats.

"I was leaving the church anyway. The decision was made the minute I kissed her. I'd wanted to the first time I saw her, you know?" He looked back at Joto and laughed darkly. "The liturgy always said, aim for love. I think I missed the mark."

"Doubt it," Joto muttered.

Michael motioned for him to continue.

"Thought you wanted me to lie to you?" Joto said. "Man, that girl's just trying to keep you from getting dead or worse."

"Worse?"

"There's worse than dead," Joto said darkly. "Think about it. She only took a small piece of your soul. Believe, had she snagged the whole thing, you wouldn't even be here. That's pretty impressive control on her part. Most times, ain't nothing but a walking shell behind her. Some of them poor bastards wander for days before they fall. Some never do."

Michael remembered the screaming, desperate souls he'd seen at The Crossroads. He shivered.

"She showed me. It was sad, terrifying. All those trapped, hopeless people. The heat, the stench."

"Imagine having to commute there for work," Joto said. "Samedi owns her, Mike. Long as she's got that spike in her chest, she goes wherever he yanks her. He crooks a finger, she's right back at the Crossroads."

"That's crazy."

Joto shrugged. "That's the Delta. You can live your whole life in sorrow and never know how blessed you are. Or walk around on top of the world, not knowing the curse you're under. No idea that right around the corner a Baron is waiting for one little fuck up he can use to make you his puppet for as long as he feels like it."

Michael lifted an eyebrow at him. "We still talking about Danni?"

"Nobody likes a smart-assed drunk."

Joto passed him another shot. Michael held the glass between his hands. "And nothing can change it?"

"Nothing I know of. Not potions or spells or gris-gris I ever found. Not even making friends with a priest."

"We didn't become friends just because you thought I could save your soul."

"No, we didn't." Joto smiled. "But it wouldn't have been a bad side effect."

"I'll get right on that. You mind if I try to help Danni first?"

"She doesn't want your help."

"Has to be some way to get that nail out of her chest."

Joto swirled the bitter ends of the bottle and turned a glass' worth out on the ground below.

"You need to be paying attention to your own chest, son."

Michael's hand went to his heart as he remembered the strange hard edge he'd felt when they had been pressed together in her room. When his hands had moved over her body and there had been... something. But his mind was on other things, softer things. All of those thoughts were washed cold by the memory of the hard, sharp pain and the suffering in the Crossroads.

There was no hard metallic spike beneath his fingertips. Not yet. Samedi could bring him to his knees without a nail. What would he do to Danni? Drag her across the underworld and back again. Forever.

Michael shook his head sadly. "All this over one stupid, little soul."

"Might be stupid, but your soul ain't little," Joto said. "Don't you forget it neither."

"Not mine, the one she took from Samedi. Whatever

got her all wrapped up in this mess."

Michael lifted the glass to his lips, but Joto flattened his hand against the rim to stop him.

"Wanna give that to me one more again?"

"She took a soul from him during Katrina. According to her, that's how she got the nail and the knife."

Joto's fingers tightened around the top of the glass and withdrew it from Michael's grasp. He set it back on the rail and twisted around toward the door.

"You might have opened with that."

When Michael pushed himself upright, the alley below him twisted like a funhouse floor. He took a minute to right himself before following Joto into the shop.

The hallway was dark. Whatever Joto was after, he was in too much of a hurry to find the light. Michael used his hand to keep himself steady as he tripped forward in the darkness.

"J, where'd you go?"

He heard Joto's chair before he saw it. The mountain of books on his lap teetered and slipped toward the floor. Michael dove to catch them then helped him lay them out against the table. Joto unfolded them at a frantic pace, flopping over the pages of one before reaching for another, muttering as he went along.

"I knew there was something wrong with that damned knife. I knew it when I saw it, and I told myself, no, Joto, she made her own deal, ain't none of your business. Be damned if I didn't see it when she walked in here flashin' up all that heat."

Finally, Michael grasped both his hands to stop him. "*What* are you talking about?"

"The *lam te mouri*! She ain't never should have had it to begin with! Look here."

Joto flopped open another book and swished past an inked language Michael couldn't even identify let alone read. He followed Joto's finger to the top of the page. It took a few tries to bring the shape of the illustration into focus. Same bone handle, same blade. Same markings.

"What do those say?"

"That's the thing," Joto said. "Ain't nobody can read it but a loa."

Michael looked at the picture again. "I'm not following you."

"Mike, she ain't like me! I made my deal, bleeding out, back in the war. The Baron gave me life, and then he gave me this chair so I wouldn't forget it. He cuts me off, I'm done. Call the parade. But if Danni snatched a piece of that magic, like you say, it's hers now. He cuts her off, she's still got it."

He could only think of one question. "How?"

"Doing magic in a storm is a fool's game, at best. Katrina now, that was something else again. Like all the magic in the Delta got pushed through an old tub washer, everything churning, twisting around. The storm dropped the Gulf on us in sheets. A whole lot of power up and washed away. Salt water can do that. It cleanses like holy water. Once the water went home, what magic was left was either pure or powerful scary.

"Man, the moon went underwater that night. Magic was everywhere, washing through the air, racing across the water like electricity on acid. There's a lot of room for 'whoops' in the middle of a hurricane. And it looks like Samedi made one."

"And that's why he gave her the knife?"

"It's why he *could*. Only thing that *can* steal a soul is a Baron."

234

"Are you saying…" Michael licked his lips and tried to form the words. "…Danni is a Baron?"

"Well, maybe not like Samedi or his brothers, but they aren't Barons either unless they've got souls. Don't you get it? As long as Samedi's got her under his thumb, he can use the magic. The nail's just his way of convincing her of that."

Michael shook his head hard and the swimming behind his eyes flooded into his stomach. Too drunk to think, he sank back into the tableside chair and dropped his head between his knees. He tried to steady his racing thoughts, but every answered question led to another.

If Danni was a Baron, could she break free from Samedi? If so, how? What did that mean for her soul? Or his?

Joto coaxed his head up again and pressed a hot cup of something into his hands. His stomach clenched and he shoved it away.

"Oh, no way!"

Joto shook his head. "Instant sober. Down the hatch."

Michael wasn't certain he wanted to be sober, but he did want the room to stop spinning. He pinched his nose and tried to ignore the taste when the closest thing he could think to match it was pickled cabbage and oatmeal.

He gagged. His stomach rose in his throat, only to be swallowed back down. The room instantly normalized, leaving him feeling surprisingly clear headed.

"Whoa," he said.

"Yeah. Remember that next time you tell me you want to forget something."

Michael followed Joto back to the table and the pile of books.

"Do you think she has any idea?" Michael asked.

Joto shook his head. "It'd be in Samedi's best interest that she don't. So, probably not."

"I have to find her," Michael said. "Where would she go?"

Joto chuckled. "You're the one who's in love with her. You tell me."

Michael wracked his brain, running over everything she'd told him in the last few days. Her apartment had burnt down. She'd already been and gone from the house in Mandeville …

His thoughts crystallized into a single word.

"Bluesland."

Michael stared toward the door with Joto at his heels. "Why there?"

"She's after the last box. Where else would it be? She's going to make a trade with Samedi."

"For her freedom?"

"No," Michael stopped halfway down the stairs. "For mine."

Thirty-Eight

Danni pulled her knees against her chest and watched
The Baron Samedi swaggered across the battered rubber
playground. He spun the gold knob of his cane inside his
fist, turned a tight pirouette, and tapped the ground. A hand
opened in the loose gravel as a body began to work itself
free of the soil. The waxy edges of a face appeared.

"Funhouse," the Baron instructed. The corpse shambled
off deeper into the park.

Danni felt sick.

Of the sixty people she remembered Samedi burying in
Bluesland, the Baron had delighted in resurrecting nearly
all of them.

The Ferris wheel made a lazy rotation, dragging a loose
section along in a circle. The cars that had survived Katrina
and then subsequent vandalism marched along to an off-
key chorus of Turkey in the Straw.

"Oh, come, Danielle." The Baron opened his hand and
made a come-hither motion with his fingers. "Let me see
you."

The center of her chest burned. The dress he'd chosen

for her was a long black skirt that fell around her ankles. The back was made of braided bone and sat flush against her spine. Danni was sure she felt as inside-out as she looked.

The Baron took her hand and twirled her once. "Lovely, *cher*. Truly, a vision."

Danni dropped her arms at her sides. "Can we just get this over with?"

The last portmanteau sat against the bottom of the slide. It hadn't taken much time to figure out where it was, even less to find it once she'd learned to listen to the sliver of Michael's soul. It had guided her along the path they'd traveled the last time they'd been here and into the center of the carousel.

The sun fell toward the horizon and pulled a cool breeze in behind it. Danni closed her eyes as she swallowed the knot in her throat. Michael's soul remained the only warmth, and pretty soon, she wouldn't even have that.

Dead leaves gathered on a wind. The whirlwind split and fell apart. LaCroix stood dressed in black, from hat to spats. A hard smile formed below eyes, as frigid as a February frost.

Samedi frowned. "So good of you to join the party."

"A true host would have something to cut the dust being kicked up by his dead," LaCroix sneered. "Allow me this small contribution to your festivities."

LaCroix lofted the cane in his hand, settling the tip against his palm. Slowly, it began to spin. Light flickered from the coal knob and sparked, arcing across the small clearing to a dilapidated refreshment stand.

Magic gathered and grew inside the small wooden structure, leaking out at every splintered crack in the paneled sides. Suddenly the front counter door flew up. An incredible variety of bottles lined the counter, wine and spirits in a hundred shapes and colors, glasses of a dozen sizes.

Samedi's chest swelled. He breezed around to LaCroix's shoulder to dust the ash from his suit.

"You know what you are?" Samedi asked. "A sore loser."

"And you're a gloating scarecrow." LaCroix eyes shifted to the shuffling forms moving off in the distance. "I wouldn't do this. It's cruel."

Danni watched as another pale arm worked its way to the surface, just a hand and then an arm, bending to claw its way free.

She nodded dimly. "It is."

Samedi's cane came up beneath her chin and lifted her face to his again. "*You* put them here."

She slapped him away. "You put them here! Your games. Your rules. None of us even had a chance!"

Samedi jerked her clean off her feet. She stumbled, flung from one Baron into the arms of another. LaCroix steadied her.

"I am sick of both of you!" Samedi spit into the dirt. "Maybe you should take her once I'm done. You're used to getting my scraps, anyway."

LaCroix's hands tightened to fists. "We both know you leave nothing behind, for seconds or otherwise."

Samedi spit again and stormed off into the park. Danni heard the frantic sounds of the dead men working the machines, chased by Samedi's screams.

She stepped back from LaCroix. "Thank you," she whispered.

"*Pour rien, cher*. It irks me to see him strut." He moved toward the bar. "A drink?"

He dropped ice into three glasses with a flourish and poured a smoky liquid from a pewter flask. He handed her one and raised the other to toast. Their glasses touched and sent a single, chiming note across the desolate park.

"Why Michael?" she asked.

LaCroix lifted a single eyebrow. "Curious inquiry to make in the moment." A white-gloved finger tapped the center of her chest. "Then again, one might ask you the same thing."

Danni took another long pull from the glass and then imagined she saw Michael's face in the shallow bottom of the glass.

"He's kind. Faithful. Honest to a fault." She chuckled. "Funny, from time to time."

LaCroix rolled his eyes. "Why then, do you think, would Michael choose you?"

Danni shrugged. "Careless, maybe."

"A careless man does not forsake all that he believes for the love of one woman, *cher*. But then, you might want to ask him."

LaCroix tossed back the rest of his glass and angled his voice over his shoulder.

"Boy, you don't learn to skulk better than that you're going to get dead."

Danni swallowed a gasp as Michael stepped out from the edge of the bar.

"What are you doing here?" Danni hissed.

Michael turned to LaCroix. "I want to use my boon."

LaCroix shook his head. "As much as I would welcome the challenge, I cannot act against my brother on his ground."

Michael shook his head. "I just need five minutes. Please. Just stall him for five minutes."

LaCroix considered him for a long moment. "Don't do anything foolish."

"Do I ever?"

LaCroix gave him a side-long look before walking off into the park. As soon as he was out of sight, Michael pulled Danni against his chest.

"Are you alright?" he asked.

She pushed him back. "I will be as soon as you leave."

Michael shook his head. "Do you want to know why I chose you, Danni? Because you're the one true thing that I want in my life." He clutched both her hands in his. "I love you. It took me a while to figure out, but I did."

"Too late, Michael. You figured it out too late."

The Ferris wheel shuddered to a halt. Metal creaked as the empty carts swung on their hinges. The silence that followed was filled by Samedi's outraged roar.

Michael started toward the portmanteau, but Danni cut him off halfway across the playground.

"What the hell do you think you're doing?"

"Leveling the playing field."

He reached the box, but she was quicker. She whipped him around.

"You can't! Don't you get it? You open that thing and Samedi keeps your soul. I didn't mean to take it, I swear, but letting Samedi win is the only way for me to give it back."

"Doesn't matter," he said. "We level the playing field, the game's over. Nobody wins."

Another roar erupted deeper inside the park. Danni raised her head just in time to see a body arc through the air toward them. It landed inside the bar with a hard crash. Glass and ice flew in all directions, and the entire thing collapsed on itself. A knobby, bare arm worked its way from the bottom of the rubble with a dead groan.

Michael jerked the knife from Danni's fist and slammed it into the portmanteau. Five hundred souls raced up and out. Light blinded them as the first wave flooded over her skin. Somewhere in the rush, she felt Michael's fingers intertwining with hers. She thought to say his name but the words were lost under the weight of his lips.

Michael hand moved to the back of her neck, and Danni lost herself in his kiss. The light faded and the voices dwindled to a low hum of anger.

The Baron Samedi trembled with rage. LaCroix stood behind him, his mouth held open on a single note of surprise.

"What have you done?" Samedi demanded.

His hand swept out. The force rocketed Danni backwards. She tumbled head over feet and then landed in a heap. Michael ran to her and then looked back at the Barons.

"Tie game. Your move," he said.

A fresh cloud of ash and smoke began to pull up around Samedi. The whirlwind clouded his face as it expanded. A funnel rose from it and traveled above the highest point of Bluesland.

Pieces of amusement park blended with hunks of wet earth. Samedi roared beneath it. The storm seemed to answer him in long, whooping howls. It changed directions suddenly and slammed into the earth with an audible thump.

Michael pulled Danni against his chest and buried his face into her hair, but all he felt was wind.

He looked up to see LaCroix standing in front of them. Rocks, dirt, trees and rusty carnival parts bladed around him and past Danni and Michael.

Samedi's voice roared across the park. Where it had been a single sound before, it was now a collection of voices, with a thousand different timbres.

"You hold no power here!" he screamed.

"Not over this land, brother. But over this man, I do."

"Not for much longer."

Both of Samedi's arms swept out. He clamped them into fists and jerked. Michael was pulled up from the ground. He lost his grip on Danni as she flew in the opposite direction.

LaCroix's hands shot out and snatched the air as well. The whiplash snapped Michael's head forward and back. Joints popped and the tendons wrenched under the growing pressure of being pulled apart. Danni's body contorted at impossible angles above him as the Barons fought for control.

LaCroix's heels dug long furrows into the cement. "You will not have them!" he screamed.

Samedi jerked his arms into his body. Pain lanced through Michael's spine. "I already do!"

A sharp voice sliced over both of them.

"*ENOUGH!*"

Thirty-Nine

Everything stopped. No wind. No wreckage. No screaming. It was as if a vacuum had fallen over them. The air was still and silent.

Cemetrie came out of the stillness, shimmering into existence. A disheveled Roben scurried behind him. Whatever damage Cemetrie had done to him, it had started with his clothes, but it certainly hadn't ended there. The hard lines of his tattoo were open gashes from his temple to his throat, the thickest of which had glassed out his eye to a hazy white.

Michael crawled to Danni. He worked his legs up beneath him and then eased her head into his lap to brush the leaves from her hair. She took a long, shuddering breath.

Both Samedi and LaCroix began protesting at once.

"He cheated!"

"I did no such thing!" LaCroix shouted just as loudly. "My man opened the last box. Victory should be mine!"

Cemetrie's voice overrode them both. "*I said*, hold!"

He pointed to the earth behind him and snapped his

fingers. Roben scurried to retrieve a folding chair from a pile of rubble and place it behind his patron.

Cemetrie scowled at him. "See what's left of that bar and make me a drink."

He sat easily and crossed his arms, beaming. "Well, ain't this just something?"

Samedi blew out a long gush of air and swept the top hat from his head before stooping to a low bow.

"The victory was rightfully mine." His eyes glowed silver with rage, sweeping over Michael and Danni and settling briefly upon LaCroix. "But someone cheated. We agreed at the outset he could not use my own player against me, even if she was stupid enough to fall for his trickery."

Michael felt a shudder pass over Danni's skin. She gasped. Michael's hand slid from her shoulder to her heart. The nail beneath her skin twisted down a half-turn.

LaCroix removed his hat and bowed, matching Samedi's posture. "I merely granted my player his boon. Nothing more, nothing less."

Samedi bristled again. "*Cemetrie*," he warned. "Do something before I do."

"What?" LaCroix snarled. "Beg for more mercy?"

"The Caribbean is not the only thing that can call up a storm worth reckoning, brother."

"Now, now. No need for that again." Cemetrie stroked his chin and considered Samedi. "Victory certainly did appear to be yours, brother," he said. He turned to LaCroix. "That is, before you left the players alone with the box."

"He left first," LaCroix pointed out. "I merely acquiesced to his insistence that I join his party."

"That is also true," Cemetrie said. "Whatever shall we do?"

Roben was working his way back to Cemetrie with a

glass cradled in the hollow of his hands. Michael caught the steely glint in Danni's eye a second before her foot shot out in his path.

All three Barons watched with equally bored expressions as Roben stumbled and then fell. He juggled the drink the entire way down but ultimately lost it beneath him. Michael heard the crisp pop of the glass followed by Danni's soft chuckle.

"Let me kill all of them," Samedi growled.

"*Hmpf*," Cemetrie sniffed then turned back to Samedi. "I suppose I must let you try."

"What?" Michael gasped.

"Each of your players failed to claim the prize. The next moves are yours against each other."

"Works for me," LaCroix said.

He passed a hand across the coal headpiece of his cane. A small whirlwind of leaves began to form around him.

"No, brother," Cemetrie interrupted him. "In accordance with the old ways, that is, man to man."

Both Samedi and LaCroix looked at him, startled.

"Unless one of you would prefer to yield the prize," he suggested.

"Never," LaCroix growled.

"Not a chance," Samedi answered.

LaCroix was first to remove his top hat and place it over the head of his cane. Samedi yanked off his coat and threw it to the ground. He dropped his hat and cane on top of it. Cemetrie waved a hand at Roben, who hurried forward to collect them.

Stripped of what made him a Baron, Samedi still looked dangerous. His skin was an unworldly shade of blue-black, as though he'd been held over a fire and then polished to perfection in some forge-god's own image. His chest began to rise and fall as he drew in big, living breaths.

Likewise, LaCroix let the change breathe and settle. He flexed his hands to fists and cracked his knuckles.

Cemetrie snapped and pointed again, sending Roben scuttling forward to retrieve Danni's knife. He set the blade against the outside of his arm. If he felt the pain, he didn't show it. His strokes were sharp and even. The skin came off in one long, glistening strip.

Samedi extended his right wrist and LaCroix mirrored him. Roben lashed their arms together with his own skin and dropped the knife on ground between them.

"This is seriously about to happen," Danni said.

"Not about to, *cher*." Cemetrie raised a knotted finger and drew a circle in air beside his head. A silver ring flared around both Barons. "Is."

Who reached first she couldn't tell. While they seemed human, their movements were anything but. Lacroix bobbed forward and back. Samedi fought for control, but keeping his head at a safe distance also prevented him from capturing the knife.

LaCroix's first blow came in hard and fast. It landed solid against Samedi's temple. It might have leveled anyone else, but Samedi shook it off and took his own shot. LaCroix reeled back and ducked under the swing, slamming his shoulder into Samedi's gut while his free hand found the knife.

Danni flinched and grabbed her chest. Michael searched her face.

"What's wrong?"

Her voice came out through gritted teeth. "The nail."

The nail twisted against Danni's breastbone again. She found fresh blood when she touched it.

Samedi locked his arm around LaCroix's throat,

spinning him into a headlock. But it lasted a second too long, and the blade disappeared into Samedi's side.

Blood flowed from the wound in Samedi's side. It ran over the length of the knife and down to the handle. Samedi wrapped long fingers around LaCroix's hand, pinning it to the hilt. He pulled and the blade raked free from his side. Blood slung in a thick line through the air.

Samedi roared and levered LaCroix's arm, dragging him off balance. He brought a knee up into LaCroix's groin. LaCroix lost his hold on the knife. Samedi's left knee rose again. He drove it into LaCroix's shoulder.

They rolled and threw short-range strikes into each other's face. LaCroix dove for the blade again, but it was out of reach. Samedi yanked LaCroix toward him, but LaCroix was ready, using the momentum to swing a heavy hand in a roundhouse that landed audibly against Samedi's left ear. LaCroix gave him no time to recover as he dragged Samedi forward.

Samedi rushed the distance with a desperate howl and drove a shoulder into LaCroix's side. Their conjoined hands came down over the blade.

Chin to chest, Danni struggled to breathe as the nail wormed its way out of her chest. Every blow LaCroix landed, resonated in another half twist of the nail as it wrenched backward from her skin.

LaCroix dove in behind Samedi's passing arm, grabbing the knife. He twisted Samedi's grip away from the hilt and then swung back, landing in squarely into Samedi's other side. He buried the first two fingers into the first wound. The blade dragged its way up past Samedi's ribs as Lacroix used it for a hand-hold to stand. He withdrew it one final time, rolled Samedi onto his back, and drove the knife deep into his heart.

Danni screamed. The nail pulled itself from her chest and bounced across the cement. She sank to her knees and then tried to rise again but collapsed back to the ground. Michael eyes darted from her face to the nail.

Danni licked her lips. "Ow."

Michael breathed a sigh of relief as she reached for his shoulder.

"Help me up," she said.

"You sure you don't want to—"

"No. *Up.*"

He led her to her feet, keeping her steady as she took the first few shaky steps toward Samedi's body. Danni lifted her foot, cocked it back, and let loose. It met the side of Samedi's face with a wet crunch.

"*Akeyi yo*, mother fucker."

She coughed up a thick wad of spit and then paused, turned her head, and spat it into the dirt.

"Hey," Michael said softly. "You might want to save some of that for your chest."

Her head spun, but Michael held her. She ran her palm across her tongue and then scrubbed her hand across the wound, watching the hole fade to a pinprick.

A hazy, half-lit version of Samedi, floated over his own body.

"Oh *cher*, kicking me while I am down?" Samedi said.

Cemetrie stood. "It is decided."

"So it seems." Samedi's hollow eyes narrowed on LaCroix. "Even a blind squirrel gets a nut. You got lucky."

"You got dead," LaCroix answered.

"Won't happen again," Samedi challenged.

"Indeed," Cemetrie interrupted them. "It may, in fact, not."

He made a short motion and Roben hurried to his side.

Cemetrie took the canes and hats and held them in front of him.

The hats went into the air and the canes slammed against the ground. They bounced off the cement, rebounding up and then smashing into each other. Where there had been two canes, Cemetrie now held one made of white ivory twisted around black mahogany. Gold and silver filigree formed three gold X's across the face of a small silver shovelhead.

Cemetrie extended his hand and caught a top hat with a gold and silver hatband and an enormous black feather. He twirled it once before settling it on his head. A little bump raked the brim to the side.

"You cannot do this!" LaCroix demanded. "I won according to the old ways."

"Indeed you did, Brother," Cemetrie answered. "The same old ways that say a Baron's power cannot be stolen. That is, unless he was willingly to lay those powers aside. Say, for a death match?"

"This is outrageous!" LaCroix roared. "We played your game and I won."

"Perhaps," Cemetrie said. "Or maybe you played a different game, and I won."

Samedi low laughter thinned to a maniacal cackle and then faded away. "You crafty, old bastard. We gave you our best tools, and you used us all."

Cemetrie nodded. He planted the tip of the cane softly between his feet and rested his hands one atop the other.

"You both have abused your power, and now you have lost it," he said. "What becomes of you, is up to you. Either begin rebuilding yourself as Barons worthy of New Orleans, or—"

Cemetrie looked at Samedi. "You can remain dead." He

nodded at LaCroix. "And you can live out your days as a human."

"Oh hell no," Samedi spat.

Cemetrie chuckled. "I thought as much. Return to your realms."

LaCroix balked. "But how am I supposed to get there?"

Cemetrie looked them up and down with a tired expression. The tip of the cane cracked against the concrete and Samedi and LaCroix vanished.

Forty

"Excuse me, Baron?" Danni swallowed hard. "What about us?"

Cemetrie chuckled and walked to where the nail had fallen. He plucked it from the pavement and turned it over in his fist.

"A long time ago," he said. "Gran Maitre created the earth and the loa. Then man. Then he split. He left the Barons to oversee the affairs of men." He looked at Michael. "Or so the story goes."

Cemetrie held the nail out to her. Danni folded both hands around it and held it against her chest. Cemetrie brushed a stray hair from her face. Unlike Samedi, Cemetrie's touch was cool and soft but as dry as dead leaves against a headstone.

"Had you made good on your deal with Samedi," he said, "I'd have to keep his end of the bargain. Since you didn't, Michael's soul is yours now. Do right by him. He loves you."

Danni stared at the nail in her hand. "What about Gabriel and the other children?"

Cemetrie smile turned lethal, all hints of mirth were wicked away by the passing breeze.

"You've won the day, *cher*. Don't get greedy."

Michael's hand pulled gently at her arm. "He's right, Danni."

"No." She stepped up Cemetrie. "They weren't yours to begin with."

Cemetrie seemed to considered it. "You'd rather them stay in Brother Samedi's care?"

"Not his either."

"Then whose, *cher*?"

"Mine."

Cemetrie rocked back on his heels and racked the cane once against the ground.

"You knew," Michael whispered.

Danni shook her head. "Not until the nail was gone. But I can feel it now."

Danni turned to Cemetrie again. "What makes a Baron, *mesye*? The power to steal souls? To protect them? I did both. Samedi sent me here to take what he was owed, and I did that. But I chose to leave the orphans of Bluesland. Since I never laid down my power, they were never Samedi's to claim. Release them to me."

Cemetrie's chin rose, defiant and then amused as he shot a look at Roben.

"You was right about one thing. She is a snotty, little thing."

He glared at Danni. "Very well, sister. They're yours."

Another low whisper passed through the park, followed by a squeal of laughter and delight. The sound passed through the heart of Bluesland, carried on the wind but echoing deep into the earth.

Danni rolled her shoulders and flexed her neck side-to-side as the air rode the length of her skin.

She nodded once at Cemetrie. "Thank you."

"Don't thank me yet, *cher*." He leaned in close enough she could smell the ash in the back of his throat. "You're in a whole new game, now."

Cemetrie snapped again and Roben hustled up behind him. He tipped his new hat to them and raised his cane.

The last image they saw was the sun glinting off the gold X's on the face of the cane.

Forty-One

A single-unit, air conditioner hummed and spit water into a coffee can resting on the green carpet. The room felt more damp than cool. Danni tapped a knuckle on the open threshold of the door.

"Well, what do you think?"

Sister Ned leafed through a stack of yellow invoices and frowned. "The second floor's a wreck. Plumbing's going to have to be redone. And the heat's gonna cost a fortune if we can't get that boiler repaired."

Danni shifted a narrow box under her arm and stepped into the room. "I asked what you thought."

She followed Sister Ned's eyes up and around the walls. Where the crown molding met the copper ceiling, the paint was sloughed in long curlicues that shifted in the lazy breeze of the overhead fan.

Sister Ned pushed away from the desk and stood. She hooked a thin arm in the crux of Danni's elbow before moving back toward the hall. She guided Danni down the row of classrooms. Most of them didn't look much different than Sister Ned's office. Horrible green carpet soaked and dried in Mississippi mud, walls cracked where they weren't punched clean through.

"None of the doors survived the flood," Sister Ned continued. "The transoms are still intact, though." She stomped her foot and the echo filled every empty space. "Wood's still solid. Walnut."

She led Danni farther down the hall to the old cafeteria. Florida windows overlooked a half-dozen, white FEMA trailers. A cluster of boys worked sticks into a soup of fresh rainwater and straw grass, while the older ones called them back to an in-progress game of baseball. They tossed their sticks aside and hurried to join them.

"How many more?" Danni asked.

Sister Ned sighed. "Enough so they've got full teams now. I've got six more on their way from Metairie. I made a few calls to some old friends in other parishes. They've all at least seen that tattoo."

Danni stared out at the children chasing each other around milk crate bases.

Sister Ned's voice was firm but reassuring. "We'll find them. And we'll feed them."

"Will we have enough, though?" Danni asked.

Sister Ned scoffed. "Christ fed five thousand with some bread and a couple of fish. I think we'll manage."

Sister Ned turned from the windows to stare at the gutted walls and loose insulation. "I remember when this place was a school," she said softly.

"Enough to make it one again?" Danni pressed.

"Is that what you really want to do?"

Danni shrugged. "If we're going to house them we might as well educate them, don't you think?"

"I do, I just… " Her eyes softened. "Love makes you eager, child. Makes you want to change the world. But it won't always be laughter. There will be tears. For them. For you. If you can't promise them the kind of love that endures, you'd be better to turn them back to the street now."

"Are we talking about the children or Michael?"

Sister Ned didn't waver. "We might just be talking about both." She leaned into the windows again. "He was my first orphan, you know? Not that his mother didn't love him, but it was held down deep inside her. The first time I saw him, I thought, 'Lord, this boy is lonely.'"

"You are the wild unknown to him, Danielle. Remember that." She guided Danni's attention back to the baseball game. "And to them, you're as close as they're going to get to a mother."

Danni shot her a wary look. "I'm still hoping you'll help me out with that."

"Wash them, teach them, that I can do. Protect them?" Sister Ned reached into the pocket of her habit and dumped a tight coil of yellow laces into Danni's palm. "That's going to take us all."

Danni shook the box under her arm. "I'm already on it."

The air was still full of summer, but fall was blending in at the edges. Cooler, spicier breezes whistled between the trailers as Danni moved to the back of the lot. Gabriel was tucked in the split-top of an old oil drum, swinging his dingy, white sneakers over the ground.

"Hey there, Flash," she said.

He didn't lift his head. "I'm not fast anymore."

"So I've heard." She pulled the box from beneath her arm and set it on his lap. "These might help."

Hope reignited in his eyes. Gabriel tore through the

brown wrapper and tossed back the lid.

"Will these make me the fastest again?"

"Not quite." Danni dropped to one knee and worked the tattered shoes off his feet. He handed her the first new sneaker and she opened the laces. "Sometimes it doesn't matter how fast you're going if your feet aren't on the right path. These will keep you on it."

She worked them onto his feet, drew the laces tight, and patted the top. His eyes sparkled as he rocked the heels together.

"They're red," he whispered.

Danni lifted Gabriel and set him in the dirt. He bounced on his toes twice and then broke for the gravel lot. He sailed over the low fence and backwards around the bases. The children squealed and Danni joined them, laughing freely.

"Now there's a sound I haven't heard in a while," Michael said.

She spun, startled. Her laughter died, but her smile did not.

"Children laughing?"

"No. You." He pushed himself away from the trailer he was leaning against. "You don't have to stop."

She rolled her eyes. "What are you doing here? I thought Mother Superior was making you wax the floors with a toothbrush today?"

He drew her hands into his and brushed a kiss across the tops of her knuckles. "Early release for good behavior."

"Mmm, hmm," she said, clearly doubtful.

"Actually, she sent me with a truckload of supplies."

"She finally decide I'm not an agent of Satan?"

His face was a clear 'no,' but he smiled anyway. "They're for Sister Ned."

"Ah." Danni walked out a few steps and thumbed the nail on the lanyard around her neck.

"Trust will come, in time. Although, she did warn me that allying myself with an *ex-con* might be a mistake later down the road."

Danni eyed him over her shoulder. "She finally told you, huh?"

"I kind of wish you would have, but, yeah. Though probably only because I wanted to keep the Mercedes."

Danni snorted a laugh. "I hope you didn't get in too much trouble."

"Nah. Cops figured it was a dump job. What nun's going to swipe a luxury car two blocks from the convent lot they park it in?"

Danni winced. "Sorry about that."

"Yeah, well, you can help me lay the new brick in the garden next week if you really feel bad. Anyway, she gave me the night off, and I was wondering…"

His voice faded. Danni turned again to find him toeing a pile of rocks mixed in the mud as a bare blush rose in his cheeks. Her eyes shot up to the bank of windows and found Sister Ned's thin outline against the glass.

Danni laughed again. "Why, Michael Belew, are you asking me on a date?"

Forty-Two

The Mississippi lapped a lazy rhythm against the rudder of the *Maribelle*. Danni held the rail and watched the wake as it faded into the silvery-blue darkness. The nail hung loosely around her neck with a piece of simple twine. She held it between her thumbs and felt a hand ride across her back and around her waist.

"Champagne?" he said.

She chuckled when the thick, green bottle came around her other side. "Depends. Where am I going to wake up tomorrow?"

Michael tugged at the nail resting in her hands. "I suppose that depends on a lot of things."

He stepped back, and Danni turned against the rail to face him. He pulled a small jewelry box from his pocket and handed it to her. "A thank-you gift from the sisters."

Danni rested the nail against her stomach and unfolded the box. A single, silver chain spilled around the face stamped in the matching pendant.

"I'm afraid I'm not very familiar with patrons of the Catholic variety."

"It's St. Julian, Patron Saint of warriors."

Danni swept her hair away from the back of her neck and let him fasten the chain in place. "Although it may be as much message as gift," he said.

"A message?"

"They're hoping you'll stay."

"They don't have a choice in the matter." The ship changed course and they rocked against each other. "But you do."

Danni pressed her mouth against his. The taste of oranges and chicory washed over him, inciting old memories and promising new ones. He heard a chorus of voices on the shore and the faint clank of a buoy farther down river. The air shifted and when he opened his eyes, the *Maribelle* was gone.

Shards of crystal rained around them and turned into gleaming sand beneath their feet. Unlike the Crossroads, this place was sweet, warm, and filled with the laughter of children at play.

Christopher Durant stooped to take the hand of a little girl. He glanced back at Michael and smiled before he lofted the girl onto his shoulders and raced off into the song.

Danni drew back from him and waited for his answer. He reached out to take the rail and sucked in a quick breath.

"*Akeyi yo.*"

Epilogue

Long time back, Gran Maitre was alone. The sun was cookin' the earth like fire round a crawfish boil. Gran Maitre was catnapping in the marsh grass while the surf kept time with his ancient heart. He drifted into a deep dream of what was to be.

He heard the beatin' of drums and the thumpin' of a big string bass. Horns blew the sun across the sky and kept right on blowing under a bone-white moon.

Some folks up and wept, drowned in their loss and longing. Others danced like it was a warm summer shower. They took what washed over them and felt it for what it was, latched on to them feelings and celebrated ever' one.

These were Gran Maitre's people.

So, in his dream, Gran Maitre' took a finger and dug a crescent line around his city. Then he spoke with a voice loud and deep. It rumbled down through time so all his descendants would hear and recognize.

"This is our land," he said. "Our island. Our people. Hold them close. For every sorrow, let there be celebration. For every pain, a pleasure. For every hunger, a feast. Do this, and they will always remember."

Things are always changing in the Crescent City. Life on the Delta isn't about the past or even the present. It's about the future and who it's going to belong to next.

Get the next book:

Dust to Dust

Prologue

1827 — Baie Chevreuil, Louisiana

Bél fanm se traka.

Beautiful women are trouble. It was his father's
favorite saying. His grandfather's and great-grandfather's
before that. How many generations of Jaackemel men had
echoed those words, Christian couldn't say, but he
suspected it had followed them from the Caribbean all the
way to the bayous of southern Louisiana, a prophecy to the
young and a curse of the old.

Beautiful women *were* trouble, but none as
troublesome as the one staring at him now. Body heat
curled off her wet hair in vaporous trails. She was lean and
long apart from the swell of her belly, which she held like
an explanation and an apology in the same breath. Three,
maybe four months along. Too far to hide it, that was for
sure, which was why they ever came to him at all.

The scent of mossy earth followed her into the
cabin. Christian tasted the brine baked into her skin, but
there was a softer, more verdant fragrance buried in her

blood, cloying like lilacs and sticky as pine. A lifetime in the bayous had taught his nose to be particular about many things: what to eat, where to tread, how to see a gator long before he set foot on its nest. But her scent called to the unique awareness inside him: the real power of the Jaackemel men.

He didn't need her history to know she was a creature of primacy and power. *Royalty.* Not born of the bloodlines of men or passed down through marriage and title, but real nobility. He scrubbed a hand against the bottom of his chin.

This was the most dangerous breed of woman. The kind who knew how to play dead when they were very much alive. A woman who would kiss you, kill you, then walk away with your child in her womb.

If that was the position she was in, Christian didn't ask.

Instead, he plucked open the laces at the base of her throat. The damp cotton nightdress let loose of her shoulders and fell to the floor. Her white skin stippled with gooseflesh as long thin hands moved to cover her more delicate parts.

Christian flicked his gaze toward the copper tub beside the fireplace and snapped. The water swirled in to fill the tub.

"Bathe," he told her in French. "You stink."

Sank up to her neck, she looked softer, less treacherous. Tendrils of red hair floated across the surface of the water, moving in and out from her body. She disappeared once, under and back up, cleansing the last of the mud from her scalp. She pulled her legs to her chest and rested her chin on her knees.

Christian drew a chair to the center of the cabin and sat, studying her, all the while hearing the toothless drawl of his father's voice:

Bél fanm se traka.

There was enough beauty in the swamp, enough mystery to satisfy a man's curiosity, and enough to do the heart didn't get caught up in wishing for something more. Christian wondered bitterly how many Jaackemel men had believed that, too. Scraping, saving, begging. The great-great-greats in his bloodline working until their fingers were too calloused to bend chanting the same, bitter curse: beautiful women are trouble.

But then, where had he come from? Where had any of them come from, if not from a woman? He'd asked once when he was old enough to understand the mechanics of such a thing. The answer he received had been a hard smack from his grandfather's cane; the curiosity quite literally beaten out of him, or at least the notion to ask again.

Now, Christian was alone. His grandfather was gone. His father, too; his body part of the waters he'd worked. The same water he'd taught Christian to manipulate, as *his* father had taught him and so on and so on.

Day in and day out he listened to the distant clamor of the city. Heard the jazz trickling its way down the river, carried on the backs of steamships. They were behemoths of the modern age, glittering with light and steam, people stacked around their rails, not even aware of the noise they produced and even less so of him, until they needed something their civilized world couldn't provide.

Certainly *they* wouldn't miss one woman.

Still, he asked, "Where is your master?"

She stared down at the child in her stomach, as if that was all the answer he needed.

She looked back at him. "Your French is good."

Hers was better, but still clearly not her native tongue. Where she'd come from was probably a much longer tale than either of them had time for.

"Will it hurt?" she asked.

"There are two things that truly hurt in life," Christian said. "Birth and death. Which one are you talking about?"

She slipped back down into the tub, letting the milky-pink water washed up to her lips as she rested her chin just above the surface. Finally, she stood, letting the water drip off the end of her hair before stepping completely free of the tub.

"Could I stay here?" she asked.

Christian shook his head.

"Then I don't have a choice."

There was no sense in adding to her shame. He stood and snapped again. Her cotton nightdress reappeared around her, clean and pressed into lines that made the swell of her stomach that much more profound.

"You always have a choice," he said. "Even if you can't see it. The choice to live and die? You make that every day. You made it coming here. Walking through that door. Sitting in that water as long as you did…"

Even as she realized her error, she was too weak to fight it. When her head slumped back and her knees gave out, Christian caught her easily. Carry enough cypress through knee-deep water, a body is nothing, especially someone so thin and soft.

He lay her on the bed and knelt beside her, letting his hand trace recesses in her face; all her body's efforts confined to one purpose. He combed her hair out until it was a brilliant, fiery wave over her full breasts.

This was not some debutante, another daughter of the admiralty coming to hide her shame. Nor would she ever be. The same world that ignored him, enslaved her. But he could make her a queen, and for that, she would always reward him.

Coming 2015

VIRTUE AND VICE

Other books by C.H. Valentino and Eldon
Hughes
Dust to Dust

For more information, visit:

www.chvalentino.com

or

www.ifoundaknife.com

Glossary

Akeyi yo: Haitian Creole for "I welcome you." A term of respect and acceptance of a loa.

Baron: a rank afforded to a loa inside their house. In the House of Ghede there are three: Samedi, Cemetrie, and LaCroix.

The Crossroads: Samedi's center of power. The Crossroads is a dark, hellish place with an endless ocean of souls who scream and lament for their freedom.

dòmi poud: (pronounced "do-mee poo'd") a sleeping powder

feme: Haitian Creole curse word meaning "bitch"

Ghede: (pronounced "Ged-day") a family of loa who control death

houngan: a man who practices voodoo

jou-jou: a voodoo spell, most of the time, of lesser power and meant to entertain.

koulev: (pronounced "coo-lev") a large creature that is half-human, half-snake.

lam te mouri: a "death blade" used to sever souls from living bodies. It is a double-edged blade with a bone handle.

loa: (pronounced "low-a") a voodoo god

mambo: a woman who practices voodoo

mesye: Haitian creole for "mister"

portmanteau: (pronounced "port-men-toe") a voodoo box made out of skin and bone.

toby: a voodoo painting that moves to tell a story

veve: a voodoo symbol associated with a specific loa.

vire-pyes: the gold coin used to control a koulev. It has two sides, stamped with the face of a man on one side, and the face of a snake on the other. When the two halves are connected, the master can communicate and control the creature.

About the Authors

C.H. Valentino lives in the metro-east St. Louis area with her husband, two dogs, two cats, and a snake. She is an eight year veteran 911 operator and police dispatcher. She whole-heartedly believes Earl Gray makes the best tea.

Eldon Hughes is a writer and a storyteller who lives in southern Illinois with his wife and their menagerie of four-legged freeloaders. He has been known to run with scissors and not get a scratch. Once.